J
551.22   Levy, Matthys.
Lev   Earthquake games,

$16.00

DATE			

EARTHQUAKE GAMES

GAMES

Earthquakes and Volcanoes
Explained by 32 Games and Experiments

EARTHQUAKE GAMES

Earthquakes and Volcanoes Explained by 32 Games and Experiments

MATTHYS LEVY AND MARIO SALVADORI

illustrated by Christina C. Blatt

Margaret K. McElderry Books

MARGARET K. McELDERRY BOOKS
25 YEARS • 1972–1997

An imprint of Simon & Schuster Children's Publishing Division
1230 Avenue of the Americas
New York, New York 10020

Text copyright © 1997 by Matthys Levy and Mario Salvadori
Illustrations copyright © 1997 by Christina C. Blatt

Book design by PIXEL PRESS
The text of this book was set in Garamond #3
The illustrations were rendered in ink on paper.

Printed in the United States of America
First Edition
10 9 8 7 6 5 4 3 2 1

LIBRARY OF CONGRESS CATALOGING-IN-PUBLICATION DATA
Levy, Matthys, 1929-
Earthquake games : earthquakes and volcanoes explained by 32 games
and experiments / Matthys Levy and Mario Salvadori; illustrated by Christina C. Blatt.
p.   cm.
Summary: Uses numerous activities and experiments to explain the forces
and phenomena connected with earthquakes and volcanoes.
ISBN 0-689-81367-8
1. Earthquakes—Juvenile literature. 2. Volcanoes—Juvenile literature.
[1. Earthquakes. 2. Volcanoes.] I. Salvadori, Mario. II. Blatt, Christina C., ill. III. Title.
QE521.3.S25   1997
551.22—dc21
96-48157
CIP   AC

To the children
of P.S. 45 in the Bronx, New York,
who first asked:

"Mario, how do earthquakes work?"

and to

Nicola, Daniel, and Maia

—M. L. and M. S.

CONTENTS

PREFACE

We expect anything else to move, but not the earth!

How could the earth, which is strong enough to support a skyscraper, shake and break up? Where do earthquakes come from? Are we ever going to know *when* and *where* they will hit? Could we ever learn to build structures capable of withstanding earthquakes?

Many years have passed since we first experienced earthquakes and we have learned answers to most of these questions—but not all. Since earthquakes and volcanoes are like natural cousins, we have added a section of this book on this other scourge of humanity.

The book is built around games and simple experiments that make a physical understanding of earthquakes and volcanic eruptions easy and fun. You will enjoy playing these games alone or with a friend; others, you may want to play with parent or an older sibling or friend. In either case, you will have a good time and also learn a lot about earthquakes and volcanoes.

If you want to know more about the scientific story behind earthquakes and volcanoes, see the authors' book *Why the Earth Quakes (W. W. Norton, 1993)*.

We hope you will enjoy reading this book as much as we did writing it, but above all, we hope that you will *never* meet face-to-face with either an earthquake or an erupting volcano.

Note: Since almost all the countries in the world have adopted a measurement system called the *metric system* or *SI,* and since this system is taught in our schools and is the official measurement system of our federal government, all the measures in this book are first given in metric units, followed by the equivalent measures in the English units (but only because they are still commonly used in the United States. See Fig. 1).

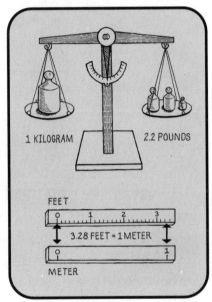

FIGURE 1

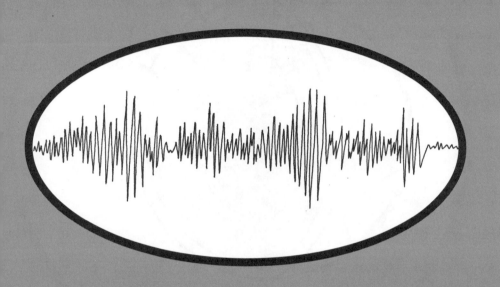

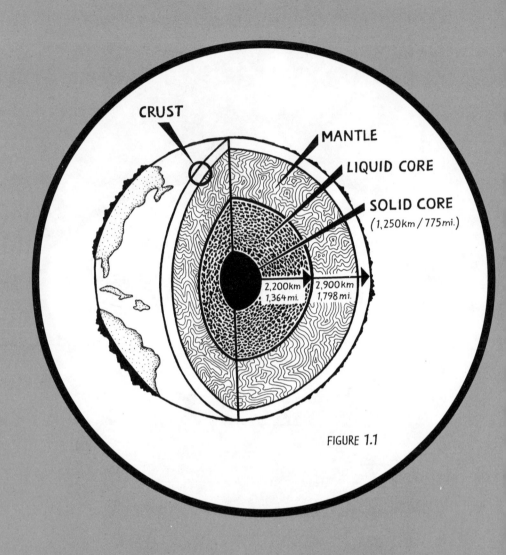

FIGURE 1.1

1

THE SECRETS OF THE EARTH

We all live on the surface of the earth, but did you ever wonder what goes on under it, deep inside the earth, deeper than the deepest mine? Of course, no human being has ever been down there; yet earth scientists have been able to learn a lot about what it's made of and what goes on inside the big sphere on which we live. And at the same time, their discoveries have helped to explain much of the mystery of how earthquakes happen and volcanoes erupt.

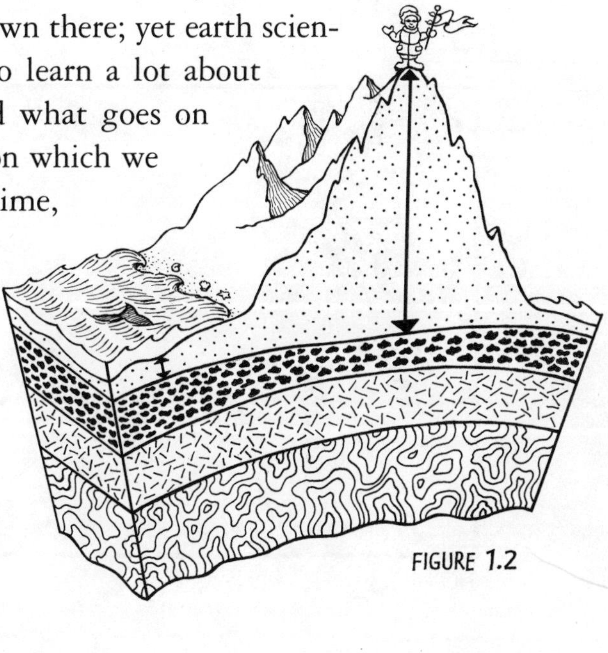

Imagine that the earth is like an apple

FIGURE 1.2

or a peach and consists of a skin, a meaty part, and a core or pit. The core of the earth is solid metal (iron and nickel) surrounded by hot liquid metals. The meat of the earth, the *mantle,* is a hot, somewhat soupy mass of melted rock called *magma.* The skin of the earth is its *crust,* the hard surface of the earth on which we live (Fig. 1.1).

The crust is not equally thick all around the earth. It is as deep as 40 kilometers (25 miles) under the surface of the continents and as thin as 5 kilometers (3 miles) under the ocean floor (Fig. 1.2).

Until a few years ago the crust was assumed to be a solid sphere of rock, but recent discoveries have shown instead that it is cracked into seven large separate sections, called *tectonic plates,* some of them so large that they determine the boundaries of an entire continent (one of them supports the entire United States!) or ocean (the whole Pacific Ocean sits on another), and many small sections that support only part of a continent or a small group of islands, like the plate under the Caribbean (Fig. 1.3).

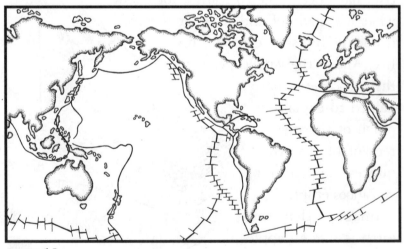

FIGURE **1.3**

THE CRACKED EGG EXPERIMENT

In this experiment you will use a boiled egg to simulate the behavior of the tectonic plates on the earth's surface.

Put enough cold water in a pot to cover an egg and bring the water to a boil. Lower an egg into the boiling water with a spoon. Turn the heat down to low and boil the egg for about 7 to 9 minutes. Take the egg out of the water and cool it under cold water. The egg should be medium cooked and not hard.

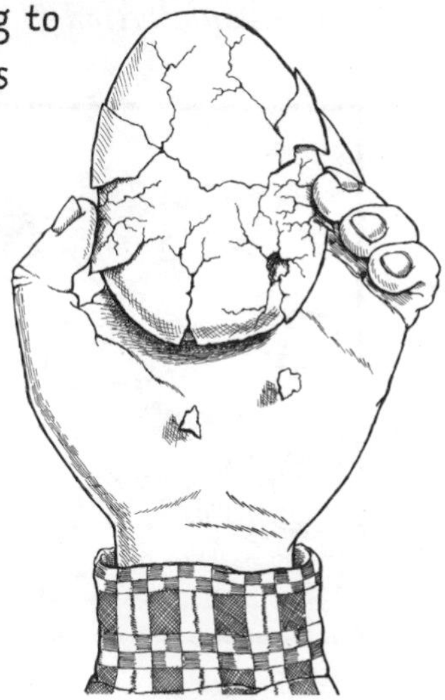

Strike the boiled egg gently against a hard surface, like the top of a kitchen table, and break the eggshell into a number of pieces, some large and some small, that will be the tectonic

FIGURE 1.4

plates of your "earth." If you now squeeze the egg gently between two fingers, the "plates" will move and some will bump against adjoining plates; others will slide along them and some will move away from each other. One plate may even slide under an adjoining plate (Fig. 1.4).

Note: Since the consistency of a boiled egg varies depending on its age, the suggested boiling time is approximate and you may have to proceed by trial and error to be successful with this experiment.

◄◄

Just like the pieces of the eggshell in the egg experiment, the separate tectonic plates floating over the magma don't stay put but move around at a snail's pace, at only 50 millimeters (2 inches) a year. As they move toward each other, one plate may hit another (Fig. 1.5a) or slide along it (Fig. 1.5b) or even duck under it (Fig. 1.5c) in what are called *subductions*.

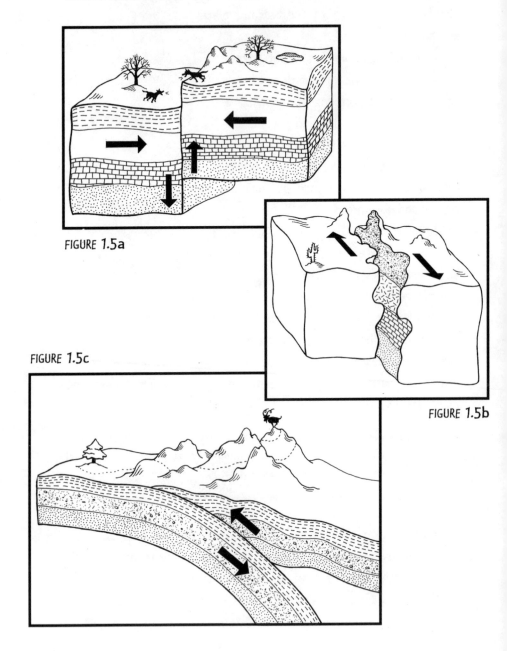

FIGURE **1.5a**

FIGURE **1.5c**

FIGURE **1.5b**

THE SCRAPING PLATES GAME

To feel how the tectonic plates bump into each other and excite earthquakes that damage buildings and kill people, you only need to use your hands.

Make your hands into fists with the knuckles bulging out (Fig. 1.6a). The backs of your hands will be your "plates" and the knuckles will represent the rough "edges" of the tectonic plates. Now push the knuckles together and, at the same time, try to make one hand slide with respect to the other (Fig. 1.6b). The harder you push your knuckles together, the harder it will be to make your

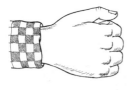

FIGURE 1.6a

hands slide; you will feel the *stress*—the force acting on a square millimeter (inch) of your knuckles—increase along your knuckles, just as it increases between the rough edges of the plates. If you keep pushing for a while, the muscles of your "plates" will start hurting because the knuckles are preventing the sliding. But eventually one "plate" will suddenly slide, releasing the energy accumulated in your hands. This is how an earthquake happens.

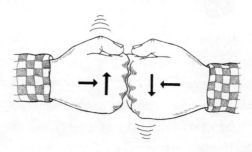

FIGURE 1.6b

◀◀

From the time our planet was first created about five billion years ago, somewhere on earth two plates under the continents have bumped and pushed against each other, neither of them giving in: they pushed and pushed, and eventually bent up the earth's crust. This is how they created high mountains and still do (Fig. 1.7). You can feel how this can happen by playing the next game.

FIGURE 1.7

BIRTH OF MOUNTAINS GAME

Keep your hands flat, with palms down, and push the middle fingers one against the other (Fig. 1.8a). Your hands represent the tectonic plates, and if you keep pushing, you will feel the energy stored in them. If you then make one hand slide under the other in a "subduction," the stored energy will be released, generating an earthquake. But if you keep pushing harder and do not slide one hand under the other, your fingers will bend up, creating "mountains" (Fig. 1.8b). The middle finger forms the highest mountain; call it

Mount Everest, or by its Tibetan name, Chomolungma, Goddess Mother of the World. It is the highest mountain on earth, at 8,848 meters (29,028 feet) high. The ring fingers represent the second highest mountain, the K^2, or Godwin-Austen, which is 8,611 meters (28,251 feet) high. The index fingers form Kanchenjunga, the third highest mountain on earth, at 8,598 meters (28,209 feet) high.

FIGURE 1.8a

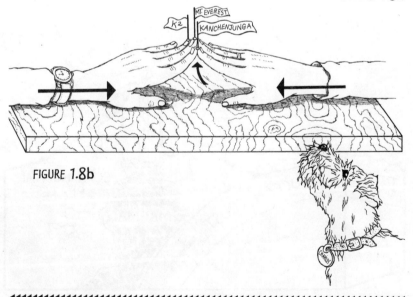

FIGURE 1.8b

Along the plate boundaries where an oceanic plate, such as the Pacific plate, dips under a continental plate, such as the North American plate, the edge of the oceanic plate plunges down into the incredibly hot mantle and melts. If a crack already exists in the crust at that point, the pressure from the weight of the crust pushes up the boiling hot melted rock, the magma, through the crack. This is how a volcano is born (Fig. 1.9).

When the tectonic plates move away from each other, most often at the bottom of the oceans, where the earth's crust is thinnest, a crack opens in the earth's crust, through which magma is squeezed up through volcanic

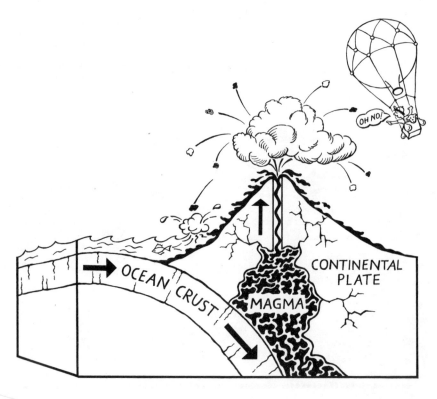

FIGURE 1.9

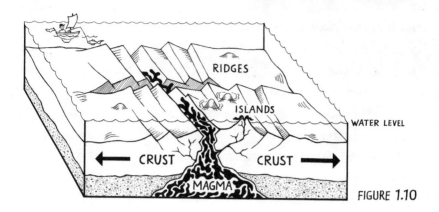

RIDGES

ISLANDS

WATER LEVEL

CRUST

CRUST

MAGMA

FIGURE **1.10**

eruptions, creating a series of underwater mountains, called *ridges* (Fig. 1.10). The one place on earth where this kind of crack passes through land and you can actually see these ridges being born is the island of Iceland (Fig. 1.11). Because the earth's crust is so much thinner under the oceans, many more volcanoes are generated there than on the surface of the earth.

At this point you may ask: "Since nobody has been inside the earth, which is so hot that whoever tried would be burned to death, how can we know so much about it?" The answer is, when two plates hit each other in a subduction, they send out *earthquake waves,* which can be "heard" just as we can hear the sound waves from a faraway explosion. Because the waves travel faster through

FIGURE **1.11**

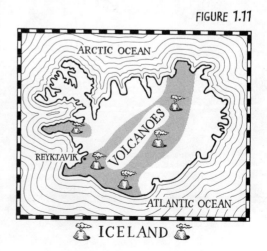

ARCTIC OCEAN

VOLCANOES

REYKJAVIK

ATLANTIC OCEAN

ICELAND

rock and slower through earth, listening to the earthquake waves has allowed the earth scientists to determine the nature of the different materials the earth is made of and to describe its composition.

Earthquakes have occurred ever since the earth's crust hardened, mainly along the edges of the tectonic plates and not all over the earth's crust. The most active earthquake areas are along the rim of the Pacific Ocean, called the Circum-Pacific belt, which starts in Japan and circles the Pacific Ocean, bringing devastation to Alaska, the West Coast of the United States, and South America, as well as Southeast Asia. Earthquakes also occur along a strip from Portugal to Australia cutting through Italy, Greece, Turkey, and Iran, called the Alpide belt (Fig. 1.12).

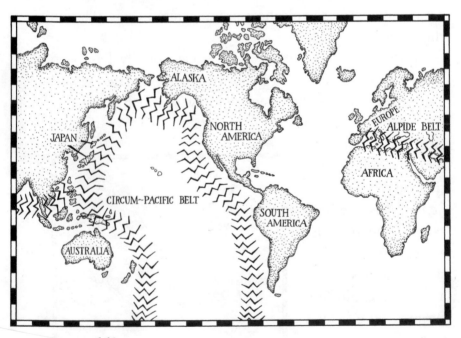

FIGURE **1.12**

THE FALLING TOWERS GAME

To show how earthquakes can damage buildings and kill people, have a friend erect two "towers" with three or four wood cubes each, on the horizontal back of one or both of your hands (Fig. 1.13a). Push the hands together as you did in the Birth of Mountains Game and suddenly let them slide against each other. The "towers of cubes" will collapse and may kill "people" (Fig. 13b). You have felt how devastating an earthquake can be!

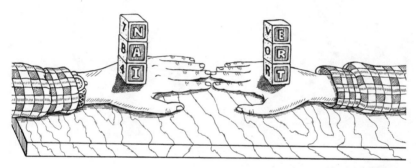

FIGURE **1.13a**

FIGURE **1.13b**

Some earthquakes are weak and do not do too much damage, but the worst can destroy entire cities and kill thousands upon thousands of people. The worst ever killed more than 300,000 people at Tangshan, China, in 1976.

At the present time most of us in the United States are lucky: strong earthquakes and volcanic eruptions occur mainly in the area of the West Coast, although in the past there have been deadly earthquakes in the East and in the Midwest as the dots in Figure 1.14 show.

FIGURE **1.14**

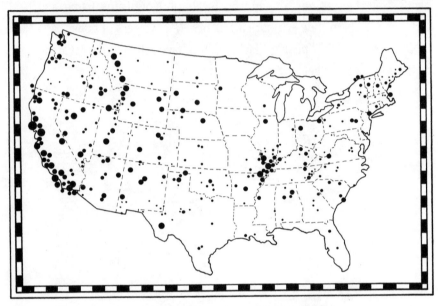

Earthquake Questions:

1. I have heard that the continents move over time. Will we, anytime soon, be able to walk from the United States to France?

Not unless you plan to live a long, long time! But you are correct, the continents are now believed to once have been all joined together into one big continent called Pangaea, which then cracked. Each section (our present continents) drifted apart and are now beginning to move together again. If that continues for another 200 million years, the continents will be close enough to build a bridge between New York City and Lisbon, Portugal.

2. If the tectonic plates are floating on the soupy magma, would they not tilt if we built all of our cities on one coast?

No, the crust is so heavy that what we build on it is like a fly on an elephant. But, as a matter of fact, the continents do tilt over time as the tectonic plates push against each other. The U.S. continent, in fact, tilts toward the east, causing the beaches on the East Coast of the United States to get smaller as those on the West Coast get bigger.

3. The book says that the magma flows out through cracks in the earth's crust under the middle of the ocean. If the magma is red-hot, doesn't it immediately harden when it reaches the cold ocean water just like melted chocolate hardens when poured into cold water?

Yes, as it reaches the water, the surface of the magma hardens, forming a crust that cracks as it is continuously pushed up by the hot magma below. The ridges that form on the bottom of the ocean, therefore, have a very cracked-looking surface.

2

IF YOU
HAD BEEN
THERE

Imagine that you were alive almost two hundred years ago. Your family was thrilled when they heard of the purchase by President Jefferson of the Louisiana Territory, an area bigger than the entire United States at that time, and they decided to establish a new home in the wilderness. You didn't know what to expect when you left your old home and friends in the city of Philadelphia and traveled westward until you reached the shore of the giant Mississippi River south of what is now St. Louis (Fig. 2.1). To begin your trek in the new territory, you had to wait for a boat to take you across the river. Finally, in early December of 1811, your father found a boatman willing to take you and your whole family across with all your possessions and even your dog, Charley.

High up on the far shore, you helped your family build a temporary shelter, where you would spend your first winter in the wilderness. While it was still dark on the morning of December 16, Charley became restless and started moaning and baying, waking you out of a sound sleep. You pushed him away to try to get back to sleep, but suddenly the ground began to groan, rumble, and shake, continuing for what felt like an eternity—and you

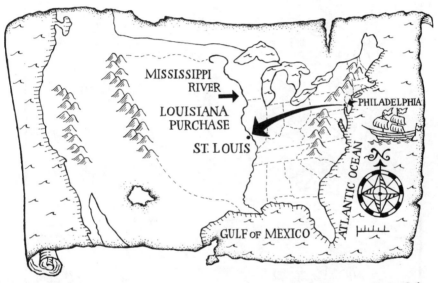

FIGURE 2.1

were scared stiff. The timbers of your lean-to creaked and the ground rose and fell as if it were an ocean wave (Fig. 2.2). Outside, you could hear the trees groan as they were bent by the force of the passing earthquake wave. While waiting for the sun to rise, you stayed huddled together with your family, not knowing what to expect next. After dawn another shock struck, and you could see the ground boiling with jets of sandy water shooting up in the air

FIGURE **2.2**

(Fig. 2.3). A crack appeared in the ground and you were afraid you might fall in it, but fortunately it closed rapidly, leaving only a scar on the face of the earth.

As you looked across the river, you saw that the steep bluff on the far side had slid down to the riverbank and that waves were sweeping up and down the river (Fig. 2.4). The boat you had crossed the river in just a few days earlier was washed up on shore and smashed. A sandy island near the middle of the river had disappeared: It had completely sunk below the water's surface.

Earthquake shocks almost as strong as the first continued for close to a month. You and your family, who had thought you were starting an exciting new life in a peaceful, virgin territory, were instead living a frightening nightmare: You had survived the most powerful earthquake ever to strike the United States. What had happened?

FIGURE 2.3

FIGURE 2.4

At this point, you might very well say, "The book explained in the first chapter that earthquakes take place along the boundaries of tectonic plates. But the center of the United States is in the middle of a tectonic plate, so how could such an earthquake occur in the Louisiana Territory?" Even seismologists—scientists who study earthquakes—cannot answer your question with absolute certainty. They believe that a deep-rooted crack exists in the middle of the North American plate and that the 1811 earthquake was caused by an adjustment of this fracture.

How come Charley "felt" the earthquake before anyone else? Animals seem to be sensitive to *precursors,* vibrations and sounds that precede an earthquake and that we ourselves cannot feel. You will be amazed by the description of the sensitivities of animals to earthquake precursors in Chapter 7.

And how come the island disappeared in the middle of the river? It did so because when sand is filled with water and is shaken by an earthquake, it *liquefies,* or flows as if it were a liquid.

 ## THE LIQUEFACTION GAME

To play this game you need a brick, enough sand to fill a pail, and enough water to just reach the level top of the sand in the pail.

First, fill the pail with the dry sand and set a brick vertically on the level sand surface (Fig. 2.5). If you shake the pail slightly, as if it were hit by an earthquake, the brick may shake but it will not collapse.

Next, fill the pail with water to the very level of the sand surface, thus *saturating* the sand with water. If you now shake the pail, as you did before you poured in the water, the brick will slowly sink into the sand,

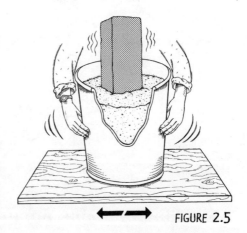

FIGURE 2.5

tilting or toppling over or even disappearing (Fig. 2.6). The brick behaves like a tall building on mushy soil and shows how the

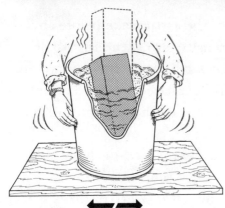

FIGURE 2.6

water acts as a *lubricant*, allowing the brick to slide into the sand. The same phenomenon takes place when a building is set on weak soil and, particularly, on soil near a sandy seashore where it is completely saturated (Fig. 2.7).

FIGURE 2.7

▶▶

Liquefaction is a very dangerous phenomenon in earthquake areas.

Earthquake Questions:

1. Our summer home on the California coast is built on the side of a steep hill. Are we safe?

It depends on whether your home is well built and, above all, the type of soil on which it stands. Loose soil may slide down the hill in a strong earthquake, but rocky soils will not (Fig. 2.8). Clay soils become soapy under heavy rains, although it is a good soil when dry. If it hasn't been done before, it may be advisable for your parents to have the soil and the foundations under your home checked by an experienced contractor or an engineer.

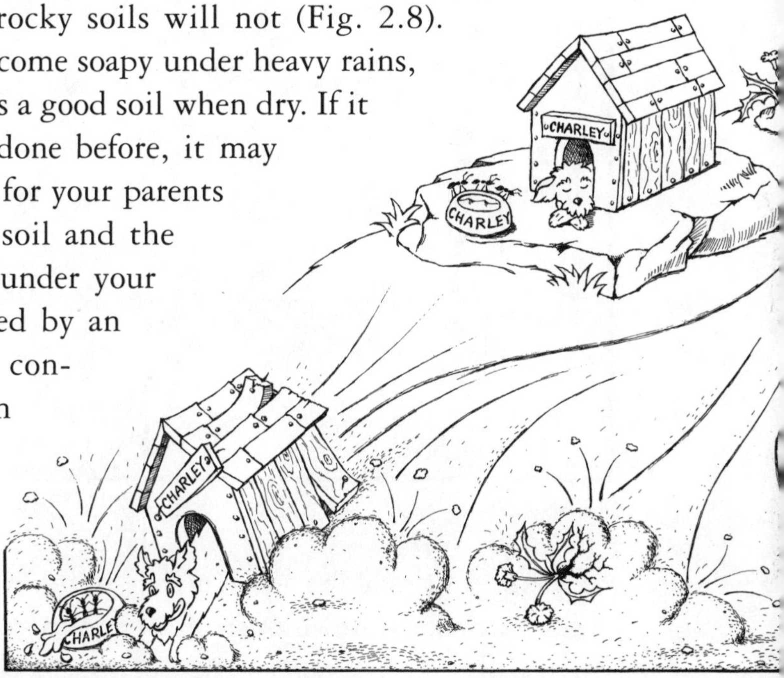

FIGURE 2.8

2. We live in Japan in a high-rise apartment building. I am nervous thinking about the possibility that our building could fall down. What could happen?

The Japanese government, and all governments for that matter, are trying to guard against something terrible

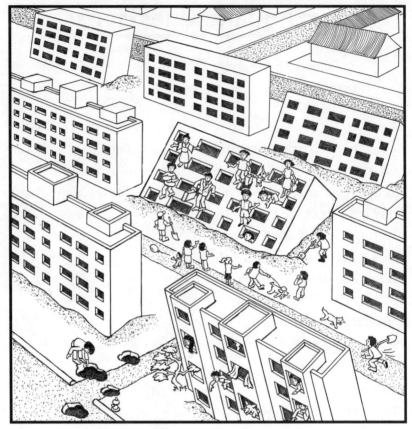

FIGURE 2.9

happening by making certain that builders follow strict rules to make buildings strong enough to stand in an earthquake. Some years ago, during an earthquake in Niigata, an apartment building built on sand that liquefied tilted almost totally on its side without breaking up so that the occupants could safely reach the ground by walking down the facade (Fig. 2.9). On the other hand, in Japan's most recent disastrous earthquake in Kobe, the earth shook so violently that many apartment buildings on soft soils collapsed.

3

WHEN THE
OCEAN ROLLS

In Chapter 1 you learned that the magma of the mantle is very hot. Because its temperature is not the same throughout the mantle, the magma develops "hot rivers" that move in circular motions, rising and falling under the earth's crust (Fig. 3.1).

FIGURE 3.1

THE CONVECTION EXPERIMENT

Place a pot of water on the stove and turn on the heat (please do this in the presence of a parent or other adult). When the water is boiling, drop a few grains of rice into the pot. Notice that the water pushes the grains of rice in a circular motion: up the sides of the pot, then away from them near the surface of the water, then dipping down to the bottom in the center of the pot, and finally back up the pot's side. The grains of rice are moved by *convection currents* just as the hot rivers of magma move around the mantle (Fig. 3.2).

Now carefully drop two pieces of 50 mm (2 in.) square toasted bread into the water. Notice that the pieces of bread move toward the center of the pot and that sometimes one piece of bread rubs against the other, while at other times one piece dips under the other. This demonstrates how tectonic plates are driven by convection currents and move about our planet, causing earthquakes when they bump into each other and opening cracks called *rifts* through which magma flows up.

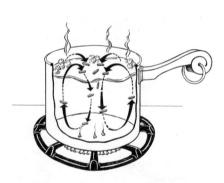

FIGURE 3.2

▶▶▶

The edges of most tectonic plates do not lie on land but under the seas, which cover over 70 percent of our planet. You have already learned that when two plates scrape against each other, an earthquake will occur. When one plate pushes up suddenly against another at the bottom of the sea, the shock pushes up a mound of water. As the mound settles down, a wave called a *tsunami* moves out in all directions on the surface of the ocean, like the waves that radiate from a pebble thrown in a pond.

▶ THE TSUNAMI-GENERATING GAME

You can reproduce this ocean phenomenon when you take a bath in the tub. Make sure the water surface is level and then slowly lower your open hand close to the bottom of the tub. Now move your hand up rapidly a short distance: You have actually "moved up" part of the water at the bottom of the tub, and you will see the surface of the water move in tsunami waves (named after the Japanese word for "seashore village wave"). You will soon learn why.

◀◀

You may at one time have made a circular wave appear on the calm waters of a pond by dropping a stone in it, and watched the wave move outward in bigger and bigger circles (Fig. 3.3). What you might not have noticed is that as the circular wave moves outward on the surface of the pond, the water particles of the pond move briefly up and down but remain where they were before you dropped the stone. You can easily check that the water particles stay put by noticing that as the wave goes by, a leaf lying on the pond's surface moves up and down, but does not follow the wave's outward movement (Fig. 3.4). This happens because a wave is a motion of the water shape, but not of the water particles in the direction of the wave.

Tsunamis, generated by the sudden changes of the

FIGURE 3.3

shape of the ocean floor far beneath the sea surface, start as waves of at most 1 meter (3 feet) high. Knowing this, and you may reasonably feel that tsunamis cannot be too dangerous. In fact, tsunamis are *extremely* dangerous because these waves are many kilometers long, and the enormous energy they receive from the snapping sea floor moves them at speeds of up to 600 kilometers (400 miles) per hour, allowing them to cross entire oceans before crashing ashore to devastate the beaches, villages, and harbors that they wash over at the end of their

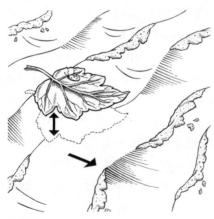

FIGURE 3.4

trip. It is because these waves smash into seaside villages that the Japanese called them "seashore village waves."

As a tsunami wave travels toward shore, it changes shape as the lower part of the wave is slowed down by the friction between the water and the sea floor, while its top, unrestrained by friction, moves faster and faster and increases in height as the sea floor slopes up (Fig. 3.5). When the wave reaches the shore, a tsunami may be a wall of water 30 meters (100 feet) high.

SEA LEVEL

FIGURE 3.5

When these incredibly powerful waves, these walls of water, finally crash on the shore, they destroy harbors, houses, and anything else in their path. If they hit a harbor, they may throw the anchored ships onto the land and destroy the docks. When they hit the mouth of a river, they run inland along the river valley, playing havoc with houses, destroying vegetation, and killing people and animals. Then the tsunami rushes back down the valley, carrying into the ocean the ruins of the destroyed villages and the bodies of its victims.

THE TSUNAMI TUB GAME

You may enjoy playing a tsunami game in your tub. To excite a tsunami in the water of your tub you will need: six bricks; many small wooden cubes about 25 mm (1 in.) on each side; a plastic tub mat; and a square sheet of plywood, about 300 mm (1 ft.) on each side.

Fill the tub with 100 mm (4 in.) of water and set two piles of two bricks each on the bottom of the tub, 300 mm (1 ft.) from the tub's faucet end, leaving a gap of 50 mm (2 in.) between the two brick piles. Place the last two-brick pile about 150 mm (6 in.) behind the other two (almost under the faucet). Set the plastic tub mat in front of the bricks to generate friction at the bottom of your "tsunami." Then build a number of "buildings" with the wooden cubes on top of the three two-brick piles (Fig. 3.6).

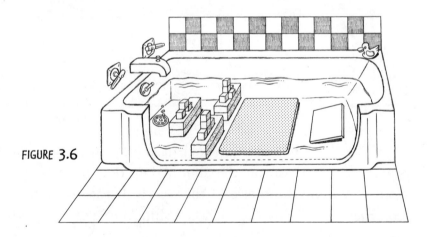

FIGURE 3.6

Now set the plywood sheet near the sloping end of the tub, slightly inclined backward, and push it rapidly forward, displacing the water in front of it in a "tsunami." Your "tsunami" will rush toward the bricks, its bottom water will be slowed down by the friction against the tub mat, and the top water will collapse the "buildings" on the bricks. It will then get through the gap between the bricks at an even greater speed and destroy the "buildings" in the "valley" behind the bricks (Fig. 3.7).

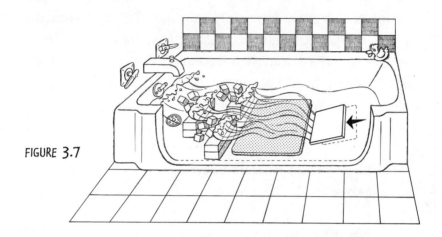

FIGURE 3.7

◄◄

This game should give you a physical feeling for the horror of a real tsunami.

Earthquake Questions:

1. We live on the coast of California. Do we have to worry about being overrun by a tsunami?

Most earthquakes along the California coast are caused by the horizontal slippage between the Pacific and the North American plates. This does not result in a tsunami. However, the coast has been struck by tsunamis originating in Alaska and even as far away as Japan.

2. How much time do I have to get away from an arriving tsunami and climb to higher ground?

Because tsunamis travel at airplane speeds, if you see one coming you have only minutes. The governments of both the United States and Japan have tried to give people more time by establishing tsunami warning stations, about 4 km (2.5 mi.) out in the ocean, which will detect an arriving tsunami and automatically broadcast a warning.

3. What happens to boats in the ocean as a tsunami passes?

Nothing! In fact, if you were in a boat, you may never even notice the passing wave because it would very slowly and gently lift and lower the boat. That is because, unlike the short waves at the beach—where you can see many crests approaching—a tsunami wave is very long and you cannot even see from one crest to another (Fig. 3.8).

FIGURE 3.8

4

EARTHQUAKE MESSAGES

The *seismic waves* of an earthquake (from the Greek *seismos* for earthquake) have told scientists what the interior of the earth is made of. These seismic waves originate at a point below the surface of the earth, called the *focus,* that may be as shallow as 3 kilometers (2 miles) in the crust or as deep as 40 kilometers (25 miles). Sometimes the focus is even hundreds of kilometers deep. The depth of the focus in the crust influences the strength of the earthquake: A shallow focus earthquake will shake you more violently than a deep focus earthquake of the same strength (Fig. 4.1).

The seismic waves originate at the focus due to the sudden slippage or movement of the tectonic plates (see p. 5) and vibrate in a variety of ways.

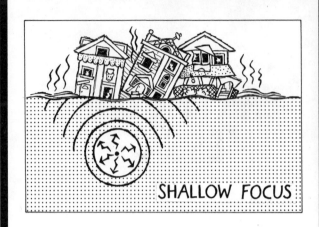

SHALLOW FOCUS

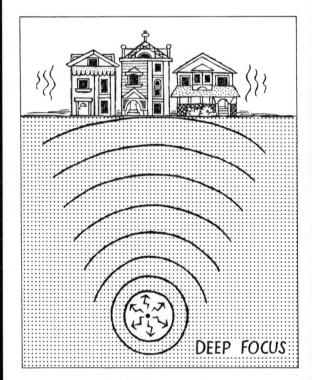

DEEP FOCUS

FIGURE 4.1

THE PRESSURE WAVE GAME

To play wave games you will need a Slinky®, an inexpensive spiral of steel or plastic you can buy in any toy store.

Set the Slinky on a table, grab one end, and ask a friend to grab the other. Pull and stretch the Slinky. Now move your hand quickly first forward and then back, and you will see a wave, called a *pressure wave* (a pack of Slinky rings close to each other) move along the Slinky from you toward your friend and then back toward you. In other words, the wave shape moves the Slinky rings (the material it crosses) in the direction of the Slinky. Because the particles of the Slinky vibrate in the direction of the wave, the pressure wave (abbreviated *P wave*) is called a longitudinal wave (Fig. 4.2).

FIGURE 4.2

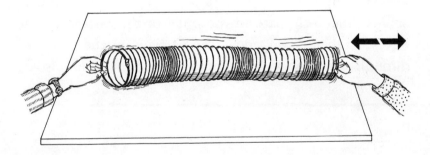

THE SHEAR WAVE GAME

While both you and your friend hold the two ends of a stretched-out Slinky on a table, wiggle your hand right and left horizontally. You will notice that a pack of Slinky rings moves to the left and right while the wave moves along the length of the Slinky. Such a wave is called a *shear wave* (abbreviated *S wave*) or a *transverse wave.* (Fig. 4.3).

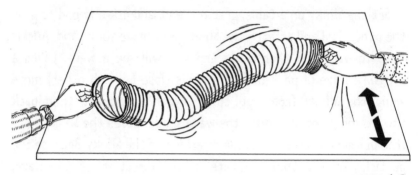

FIGURE 4.3

▶▶▶

Earthquakes emit two types of waves from the focus, pressure and shear waves, both called *body waves,* presumably because they originate in the body of the earth. Seismic waves, as they travel, move the particles of the materials through which they move and, as with the Slinky, some

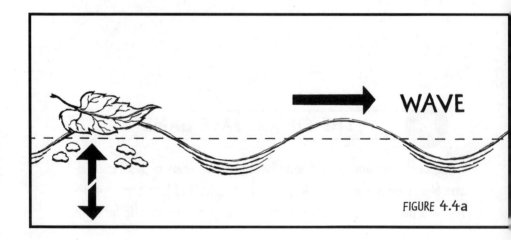

FIGURE 4.4a

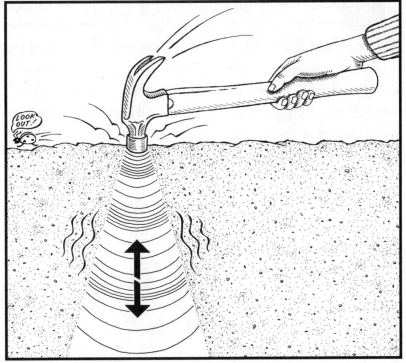

FIGURE 4.4b

move them at right angles to the direction of the wave motion, either vertically, like the water surface of a pond into which a pebble has been thrown, or horizontally (Fig. 4.4a). Others move them back and forth in the direction of the wave motion, like the waves radiating from a hammer blow on rock (Fig. 4.4b).

When these two types of body waves reach the earth's surface they give rise to *surface waves,* which are again of two types that act exactly like pressure and shear waves and that earth scientists named *Rayleigh waves* and *Love waves,* after two famous nineteenth-century British scientists.

THE WAVE SPEED GAME

Attach one end of a length of string to a door handle and hold the other end in your hand. Move your hand up and down or sideways and you will see shear waves moving along the length of the string. Now hold the line tightly with one hand and pluck the string with your other hand. You will again see shear waves moving along the string, and the tighter you pull the string, the faster the waves will move.

▶▶

Not all waves travel at the same speed. Pressure waves are the fastest to reach the surface of the earth from the focus. Shear waves travel at about half the speed of P waves, and surface waves travel at about the same speed as shear waves. But all seismic waves travel very fast: the slowest, the surface waves, travel at about 3 kilometers (2 miles) *per second* (about fifteen times faster than the speed of our fastest jetliners). The speed of the seismic waves depends on the type of material they cross: They move faster across hard rock and slower across weak soils, just as you can run faster on a hard pavement than through a muddy field.

THE REFLECTION GAME

Look at yourself in a mirror: What you see is a *reflection* of the light waves that bounce off your body (after all, if it were dark you would not see yourself). Now hold a hand mirror in front of your face while your back faces a wall mirror. As you turn your body, you can find a position where you can see a reflection of your back, with your face showing in the hand mirror (Fig. 4.5). Try to explain how the light waves are bouncing around to create such a double image.

FIGURE 4.5

THE REFRACTION GAME

Dip a straw in a partially filled glass of water and look at it from the side. At the level of the top of the water, the straw appears

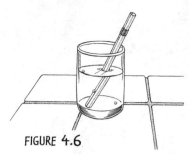

to be bent (Fig. 4.6). This apparent bending is due to the phenomenon of *refraction.* The visual waves from the straw travel at different speeds in the air and in the water, and the straw seems bent because of this difference in speeds.

FIGURE 4.6

▶▶▶

When seismic waves cross from one kind of material to another, they may change direction, in which case we say that they are *refracted* like the straw in the glass of water, or can be *reflected,* like our image in a mirror.

 # THE STRENGTH OF WATER GAME

Fill a glass with water. Take a plastic knife and plunge it into the water (Fig. 4.7a). You note that the water offers no resistance to

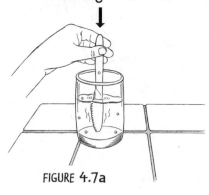

your action. Now, move the knife sideways against the broad side of the knife (Fig. 4.7b). Notice that it takes some effort to push it back and forth. This demonstrates that water has compressive strength but has no shear strength.

FIGURE 4.7a

◀◀◀◀◀◀◀◀◀◀◀◀◀◀◀◀◀◀◀◀◀◀◀◀◀◀◀◀◀◀◀◀◀◀◀◀◀◀◀

Shear waves have an additional important property: They cannot travel through liquids and, in particular, through water. That is because water has no shear resistance so the wave behaves as if there were nothing there. Luckily enough, this property of S waves, as well as the difference in speed between P and S waves, is most

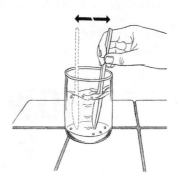

FIGURE 4.7b

useful in determining the location of the focus of an earthquake, while the refraction and reflection of the waves tell us much about the nature of the soils they cross.

Earthquake Questions:

1. The book said in Chapter 1 that the interior of the earth, the mantle, is very hot—in fact, hot enough to melt rock—and now the book says that S waves cannot travel in a liquid. Yet S waves travel through the mantle. How come?

The soupy rock of the mantle is under huge pressure from the weight of the crust above it and, as a result, its melting temperature is much greater than it would be on the surface of the earth, just like the temperature of steam in a kitchen pressure cooker is much greater than it would be in the open air. Because it is under such tremendously high pressure and has a high melting temperature, the mantle therefore feels like a solid to S waves.

5

HOW STRONG
WAS IT?

Since you are interested in earthquakes, you may have heard on TV and radio or from your parents announcements like: "Yesterday at 4:00 A.M. an earthquake measuring 4 on the Richter scale was felt in Long Beach, California. No deaths have been reported and only minor damage to buildings has occurred"; or: "Today at 4:30 P.M. an earthquake of Richter magnitude 7 hit San Francisco, killing one hundred people and causing millions of dollars worth of damage." You gather from such announcements that the Richter scale 4 earthquake in Long Beach was a weak earthquake, but the Richter scale 7 earthquake in San Francisco was devastatingly strong. What is the meaning of the numbers on the Richter scale?

Almost three hundred years ago *seismologists,* the scientists who study earthquakes, started recording the impact earthquakes had on people and buildings. These records were not well organized, so at the beginning of our century the Italian seismologist Giuseppe Mercalli suggested a standard list based on the amount of damage done to buildings and on the reaction of people to earthquakes. This is now called the *Modified Mercalli scale* and defines twelve levels of damage. But the opinions of witnesses are very personal and, hence, can be widely different. To be thrown out of bed by an earthquake may be a terrible experience for an American to whom this is happening for the first time, while it is nothing extraordinary to a Japanese who has had a number of such experiences. A better way of estimating an earthquake's strength had to be found.

And this is what the American seismologist Charles Richter did in 1935 by proposing to estimate the strength of earthquakes by scientifically measuring both the motions of the earth's crust during an earthquake and the energy of the earthquake shock.

You may ask: "And how did Mr. Richter get his earthquake scale to measure the earth's crust motions and the energy of an earthquake?" He did it by means of a measuring instrument called a *seismograph* (Fig. 5.1). Before

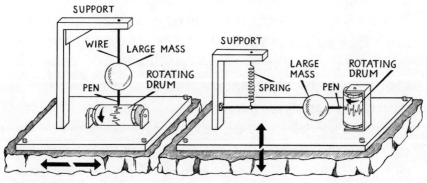

FIGURE 5.1

we explain what it is, we must introduce you to an instrument first used by Chinese scientists almost two thousand years ago that creates a picture of the earth's motions. It is called a *seismometer.*

 ## BUILD A SEISMOMETER GAME

To measure the motions of an earthquake, you need three seismometers: two of the same type to measure the horizontal motions, both front and back and left and right, and another type to measure the vertical, or up-and-down, motions of the earth's surface.

To build the two types of seismometers you will need: two large cereal boxes; two sheets of cardboard about the size of a cereal box; two plastic or cardboard cups with covers; two pencils; a pair of scissors; two strips of paper about 50 mm (2 in.) wide by 600 mm (2 ft.) long; a piece of string; a few rubber bands; two small sticks (the size of matches) and some sand. (To build a seismometer, you may want to get help from an adult or an older friend.)

To build the first type of seismometer, which measures the horizontal motions of the earth's surface, cut a large rectangle out of both large sides of a cereal box, leaving 25 mm (1 in.) wide edges. Then cut in the middle of the bottom edges two narrow horizontal slots a little more than 50 mm (2 in.) wide, through which you can slide one of the paper strips you have prepared (Fig. 5.2). Now pierce a hole at the center of the top cover and another at the bottom of a cup and push a pencil, point down, through the two holes. Fill the cup with sand (Fig. 5.3a). Thread the string through two holes near the top of opposite sides of the cup (Fig. 5.3b). Hang the cup from the center of the top of the cereal box by tying the string around a small stick at the center of the box top. Adjust the length of the string so

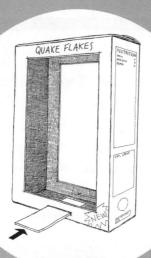

FIGURE 5.2

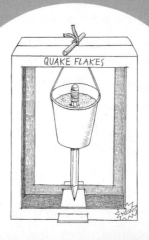

FIGURE 5.3a

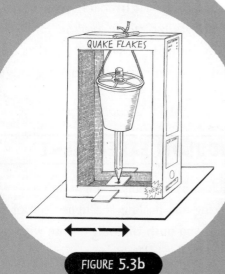

FIGURE 5.3b

that the tip of the pencil touches the strip of paper you have threaded through the bottom cuts in the box. Glue the bottom of the cereal box to one of the large sheets of cardboard. Notice that if you now move the cardboard sheet back and forth, the weighted pencil stays put and makes a mark on the paper strip you have passed through the cardboard base. Congratulations, you have built your first seismometer!

▶▶

How does a seismometer work? It takes advantage of a property called *inertia,* which is common to anything with weight, that is, to any mass. Inertia shows that the basic property of a mass is to be lazy. If it is moving, it refuses to move faster or slower unless pushed or pulled by a force. If it is at rest, it will stay put unless pulled or pushed by a force. A moving car will keep on moving unless slowed by the application of a brake force, and it will move faster only when pushed by higher engine speeds. You may have observed that a spinning top, if pushed, does not fall but comes right back to a vertical position. This is because of its *rotational inertia.*

What you have built by hanging a weight (in this case, the sand-filled cup) from a string is a fascinating device called a *pendulum.*

 THE PENDULUM EXPERIMENT

You can easily build a pendulum by hanging a weight (a stone or a heavy steel bolt) from a string and holding the upper end of the string in one hand (Fig. 5.4). If you push the weight once with your other hand, it will swing back and forth. While doing this, look at the second hand of a watch or clock and see how long it takes for the weight to move from the extreme left to the extreme right and back again. This interval of time is called the *period* of the pendulum. If you lengthen the string, you will notice that the period becomes longer (Fig. 5.5a), and if you shorten the string, the period will become shorter (Fig. 5.5b).

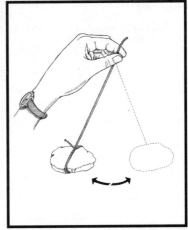

FIGURE 5.4

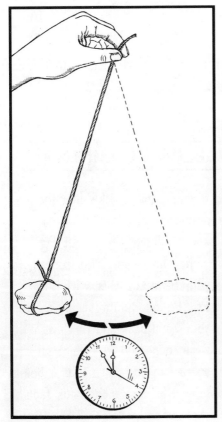

FIGURE 5.5a

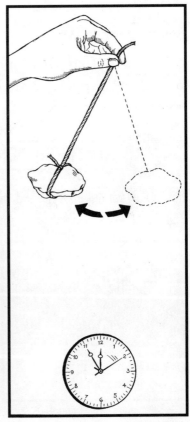

FIGURE 5.5b

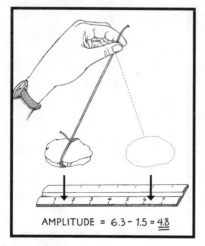

AMPLITUDE = 6.3 - 1.5 = 4.8

FIGURE 5.6

Now have a friend hold a ruler horizontally at the level of the hanging weight and repeat the swinging experiment. Ask your friend to tell you the measurement indicated on the ruler as the pendulum swings to the extreme left and when it swings to the extreme right. By subtracting the smaller from the larger number, you have measured the *amplitude* of the movement (Fig. 5.6).

▶▶

You will find that both period and amplitude are important properties that measure how fast and how strong an earthquake is.

▶ ANOTHER PENDULUM EXPERIMENT

Hold your pendulum still and move your hand, quickly but slightly, right and left. The inertia of the weight will prevent it from moving

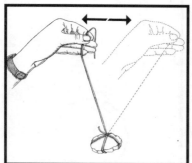

FIGURE 5.7

and it will stay almost put (Fig. 5.7).

Now hold a pencil horizontally in your hand together with the top of the pendulum string. Shake your hand back and forth as if it were connected to a point on the surface of the earth that is being moved by an earthquake. Tape a sheet of paper to a wall. Start your "earthquake" by moving your hand fast enough to prevent the weight from moving; touch the pencil to the top of the paper and slowly move your hand downward (Fig. 5.8). The pencil will draw a graph of your hand's motion that is similar to a graph measuring the movement of the earth's crust due to an earthquake. Since the weight stays put while your hand, representing the earthquake, moves, you have created a simple instrument that measures the earth's seismic motion with respect to a fixed point!

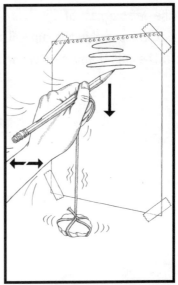

FIGURE 5.8

So far your experiments have simulated how much the earth moves during an earthquake, but we really would also like to know how fast it moves and over what length of time. When you measured the period of the pendulum, you used a clock or watch to tell you how long the motion took. By adding the measure of time, we can now convert our seismometer into the instrument called a seismograph.

 ## THE SEISMOGRAPH GAME

Shake the "earth" cardboard base of your seismometer back and forth with one hand in the direction parallel to the large sides of the box while at the same time slowly but steadily sliding the paper strip with your other hand (Fig. 5.9). The pencil will draw the *seismogram* of the "earthquake" because while you shake the box, the pencil in the cup will stay put due to the inertia of the sand in the cup. If you measure with a watch the time you have shaken

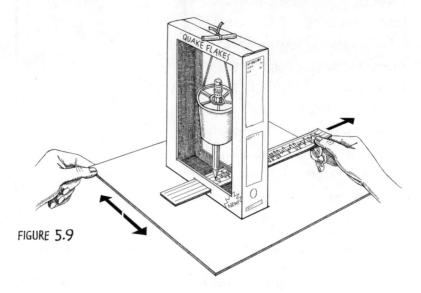

FIGURE 5.9

your "earthquake," you can draw a line down the paper strip and mark seconds by dividing the length of the graph by the duration of the "earthquake." You have thus obtained the graph of your earthquake motions against time and have a working seismograph (Fig. 5.10).

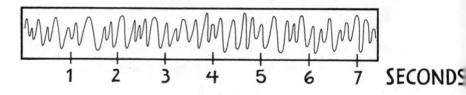

FIGURE 5.10

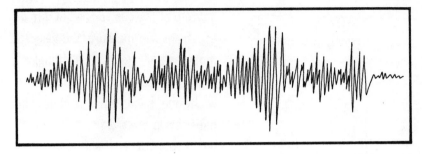

FIGURE 5.11

After you learn to shake the box skillfully, you may try to imitate the graph of Fig. 5.11, which represents the horizontal seismogram of a real earthquake.

Note: Unless you have four hands, you may need to ask a friend to be your timekeeper.

To build the second kind of seismograph, which measures the vertical movements of the earth due to an earthquake, cut a large rectangle from both large sides of the other cereal box and cut small vertical slits for the 50 mm (2 in.) wide paper strip near the edge of two opposite narrow vertical sides of the box, right next to the cut vertical large sides of the

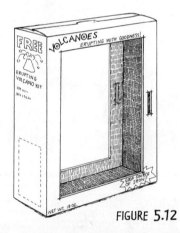

FIGURE 5.12

box (Fig. 5.12). Fill the second cup with sand and thread the pencil horizontally near its top through two holes. Hang the cup from the center of the top of the box with two rubber bands tied at the top to a stick and at the bottom to the two projecting ends of the pencil. Adjust the pencil so that it touches the horizontally sliding paper strip (Fig. 5.13). Stabilize the cup by tying a cut-open rubber band from the

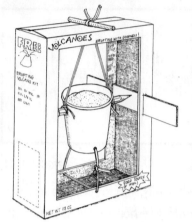

FIGURE 5.13

bottom of the cup to the bottom of the frame. To measure the vertical motions of your "earthquake," shake the cereal box up and down with one hand, while sliding the paper strip toward you horizontally with your other hand (Fig. 5.14). Graph the seismogram of the vertical motions versus time as you have done with the seismogram for the horizontal motions. (Measure the time it takes to move the strip of paper and marked it on the strip.) The pencil in the box will stay put because of the inertia of the sand-filled cup and will graph the seismogram while you shake the box up and down.

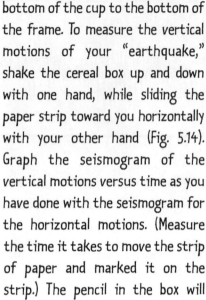

FIGURE 5.14

▶▶

Using the measurements from a seismograph, Dr. Richter developed a scale defining the magnitude of an earthquake. In order to grasp the meaning of the numbers of the Richter scale, you must become acquainted with its two main features. First, the Richter magnitude scale assigns a value of 1 to a barely felt earthquake and goes up to a value of about 9 to the strongest earthquake. So far, the strongest quake ever registered had a value of about 9, but the seismologists do not believe that an earthquake much stronger than 9 has a chance of ever occurring.

Second, an increase of 1 in the numbers of the Richter scale of ground motion means an increase of 10 in the motions of the earth's crust (Fig. 5.15). (Mathematicians call such scales *logarithmic scales* with base 10.) In the hypothetical examples of the Long Beach and the San Francisco earthquakes at the beginning of this chapter, the San Francisco earthquake of Richter scale 7 is three numbers higher than the Long Beach earthquake of Richter scale 4. Hence, the San Francisco earthquake shook the earth's crust 10 x 10 x 10 or one thousand times more than the one at Long Beach, and, of course, did much greater damage.

Seismographic stations have now been established all over the world to measure the strength of earthquakes. These stations can also be used to pinpoint the location of an earthquake by remembering that the two main types of seismic waves travel at different speeds. Measuring the difference in the arrival times of P and S waves, the distance from the focus of the earthquake to the seismograph

MOVEMENT OF THE EARTH'S CRUST

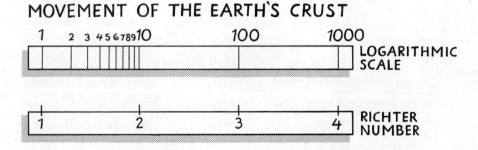

FIGURE 5.15

station can be calculated. By using the reports of the arrival time of the P and S waves from three different seismograph stations, the exact location of the earthquake can be pinpointed (Fig. 5.16).

FIGURE **5.16**

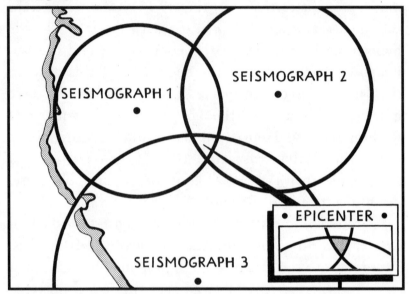

Earthquake Questions:

1. Can you help me to visualize what the Richter scale really means?

Think of the magnitude scale being represented by the volume of a series of balls. If you start with a marble to represent a magnitude 1 quake, a magnitude 3 quake will be a golf ball, a magnitude 4 will be a baseball and a magnitude 5 will be a soccer ball (Fig. 5.17).

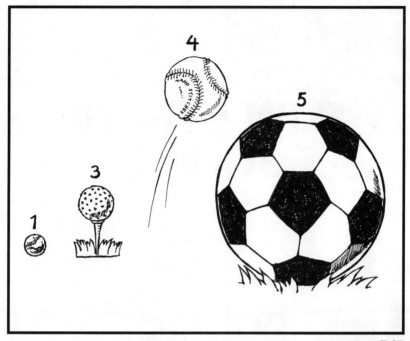

FIGURE 5.17

2. I heard that not too long ago (before I was born), a strong earthquake struck Alaska where I live. How bad was it?

In 1964 a magnitude 8.4 quake, centered in Prince William Sound, caused tremendous damage to Anchorage. It was the strongest quake to hit the North American continent in over one hundred years, and since its focus was under the sea, it spawned a major tsunami that overran beaches and harbors as far away as Hawaii and California. In fact, the quake was so powerful that even Cuba, more than 6,400 km (4,000 mi.) away, shook slightly.

6

FROM MYTH TO SCIENCE

Somewhere on earth, in the time it takes you to read this sentence, there will be an earthquake. You will not be aware of it because it may well have struck somewhere under an ocean, as the oceans cover over 70 percent of the earth's surface; or it may have hit some uninhabited part of the world; or, most likely, it was too weak to be felt by humans. Only fish in the oceans, animals on land, and maybe even the plants were witnesses to the quake. If it had been a strong one, which happens only at most six times a year, it would have been reported in the news and you might have seen its impact on television. A super earthquake, of magnitude above 8, happens about once a year, and you would certainly have heard of it because even if its origin was in the ocean or in some uninhabited place, it would have been felt in a town or city occupied by people.

THE SHAKING GAME

You will need a friend to help you with this game. Get two rolling pins, the kind used to make pie crusts and cookies, and a board the same width as the length of the rolling pins and about a meter (3 feet) long. Put the rolling pins on the floor and place the board on top of them so that the ends of the board overhang the pins by about the width of a hand. Carefully stand on the board with your feet slightly apart for stability (Fig. 6.1). Have your friend

FIGURE 6.1

grasp one end of the board and pull it very slowly, no more than 50 mm (2 in.), and push it back equally slowly to the starting point (Fig. 6.2).

Notice that if the board is pulled and pushed very, very slowly, you do not feel the movement.

Have your friend look at a watch or clock and count the number of times in a minute he or she pushes and pulls the board, thus concluding one complete movement, called a *cycle*. The number of cycles per minute that your friend records is the *frequency* in cycles per minute of the movement of the board.

Now have your friend move the board faster and record

FIGURE 6.2

the frequency, noting the frequency when you first sense the movement by feeling unsteady.

Be careful, because if your friend pushes and pulls the board very fast, you will fall off...as you would fall down in a very shaky earthquake.

▶▶

Perhaps because animals are more sensitive to earthquake vibrations and respond to even the slightest shaking, people all over the world believed for centuries that animals were responsible for earthquakes.

In the mythical tales of the inhabitants of southern Russia, a giant bull living under the earth's surface was said to be the cause of earthquakes (Fig. 6.3). In southern Chile an old legend attributed earthquakes to the fighting between two snakes, one who dug holes to store water in the earth and another who filled the holes with stones to prevent the first from storing the water (Fig. 6.4). In ancient China the winged dragon-snake Lung shook the earth on its horns (Fig. 6.5), and in India an elephant-god was the cause of earthquakes (Fig. 6.6).

TOP: FIGURE 6.3
BOTTOM: FIGURE 6.4

A frog did it in Central Asia (Fig. 6.7), and in Japan it was caused by the thrashing of *namazu,* a giant catfish (Fig. 6.8). In the Kamchatka peninsula of northern Asia, an underground dog was responsible for the earth's tremors (Fig. 6.9), and in Mexico a jaguar (Fig. 6.10). The bull of Knossos shook the Greek island of Crete (Fig. 6.11), and a goddess shook ancient Babylon, today's Iraq (Fig. 6.12). The members of certain Native American nations believed that the earth was supported by a giant tortoise and that whenever the tortoise took a step, the earth trembled (Fig. 6.13).

Modern science has at long last explained that earthquakes are due to the motions of the tectonic plates (see p.5), not to mythical animals. But so far seismologists have only been able to answer the first of the two questions concerning us most: They can predict where the next earthquake will hit, but when an earthquake will hit a specific area is a question that still baffles them.

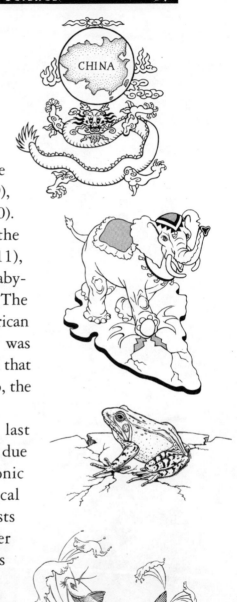

TOP TO BOTTOM: FIGURES 6.5, 6.6, 6.7, & 6.8

Seismologists believe that the location of all future earthquakes will eventually become predictable, thanks to the worldwide network of seismographic stations capable of sensing the weakest precursor shocks (the small vibrations resulting from the realignment of the tectonic plates just before a major slippage. Yet, at the present time (1997), the best seismologists can do is to predict the chance that an earthquake will occur within a time period of thirty years. One of their announcements may state, for example, that there is a 90 percent chance that a strong earthquake, maybe the Big One, will occur in Southern California within thirty years, an important but not totally reassuring piece of information for the citizens of Los Angeles.

TOP TO BOTTOM: FIGURES 6.9, 6.10, 6.11, 6.12, & 6.13

THE PREDICTION EXPERIMENT

Suppose you were an earthquake scientist and you had made a list of earthquakes and the dates of their occurrence. As you look at the list, you notice that the city of Parkfield, California, seems to have had a large number of moderate earthquakes, and you make a startling observation. You write down the dates of all the Parkfield quakes that have been reported and compute the number of years between each quake:

YEAR OF OCCURRENCE	INTERVAL IN YEARS
1857	
	24
1881	
	20
1901	
	21
1922	
	12
1934	
	32
1966	
TOTAL	109

Dividing the total number of interval years, 109, by the number of intervals, 5, you obtain an average interval of exactly 21.8 years (or approximately 22 years). Being a clever person, you decide that you can make a prediction based on the recurrence interval, and you figure out that the next earthquake in Parkfield will occur in 1988 (1966 + 22). But since you are an *extremely* clever person, you also note that there was as little as 12 years and as much as 32 years between earthquakes, so you modify your prediction: It is probable that there will be an earthquake sometime between 1978 (1966 + 12) and 1998 (1966 + 32) in Parkfield.

◀◀◀

In the hope of being able to give sufficient warning to the local population, the Parkfield area has been covered with the most sensitive instruments capable of detecting the weakest precursor shocks that, most of the time, precede a strong earthquake. It is these signals that we believe are felt by animals.

Guessing the arrival time of future earthquakes by studying the record of past earthquakes is called *extrapolation*. Whenever the faults (the cracks produced in the earth's crust by the tectonic plate motions) reach the surface of the earth, seismologists can "read," by looking at the side of the crack, when the plates moved and how much they moved due to earthquakes that occurred from prehistoric times until today (Fig. 6.14). This has been done along one of the longest superficial faults (one that

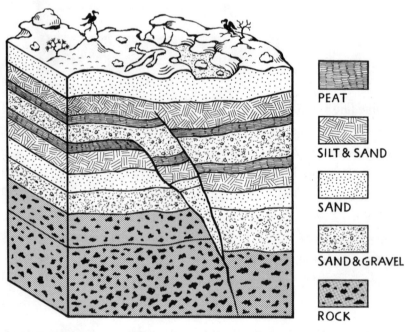

PEAT

SILT & SAND

SAND

SAND & GRAVEL

ROCK

FIGURE **6.14**

CALIFORNIA

FIGURE 6.15

SAN FRANCISCO

SAN ANDREAS FAULT

PACIFIC OCEAN

LOS ANGELES

left a trace on the earth's surface), the 1220-kilometer-(756-mile-) long San Andreas Fault near the California coast (Fig. 6.15).

Another recent approach to earthquake warning, adopted first in China and now in Japan and the United States as well, consists in gathering information about the minor phenomena that often precede an earthquake. Besides the weak precursor shocks you already learned about, changes of water levels in lakes and wells, temperature changes in the depth of the crust, and even changes in the speed of P and S waves (see p. 33) may help predict an earthquake. With the help of sensitive instruments capable of measuring these minor changes, seismologists may be able to forecast an earthquake quite accurately, as they have already done in 1973 in the Adirondack Mountains of New York State, where they were only one day off in predicting the arrival time of an earthquake. (They did it by measuring the small changes in the speed of the precursor P and S waves.)

On the basis of records dating back about two hundred years, a seismic risk map of the United States is published by the U.S. Geological Survey, in which five types of regions labeled 0–4 identify the strength of the earthquakes to be expected. The 0 areas are those that have never suffered earthquakes, that is, the safest. Areas that have experienced earthquakes of increasing strength are labeled 1 to 4 (Fig. 6.16).

FIGURE **6.16**

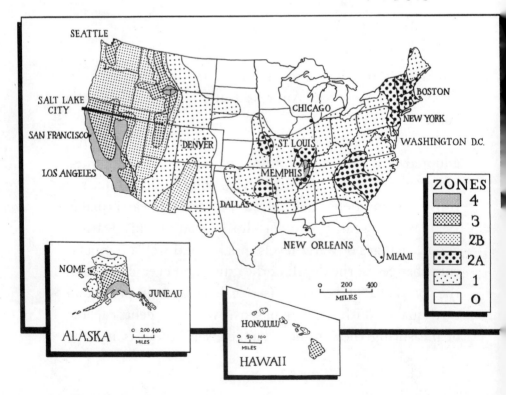

THE RISK GAME

On the risk map in Figure 6.16, first locate the state in which you live and then try to pinpoint your home town. You will then be able to tell which zone you live in. If, for instance, you live in Memphis, you are in zone 3, which carries a serious risk of earthquakes. On the other hand, if you live in New Orleans, you need not be concerned because you are in zone 0. If you study the map, you can also locate the homes of your friends and family and determine their earthquake risk.

◀◀

We will explain later what precautions you can take to prevent injury if an earthquake is expected in your area.

Earthquake Questions:

1. Are there maps that will identify the risk of earthquakes in countries other than the United States?

    Every country has its own maps and often uses different numbers to represent the intensity of earthquakes. Japan, for instance, has a magnitude scale that goes from 0 to 7, compared to the Richter scale that goes from 0 to 9.

2. I live in Missouri and our teachers make us drill against earthquakes, but we haven't had any since I started school six years ago. What's the purpose of these stupid drills?

    Earthquakes hit when you least expect them. We suggest you take these drills very seriously: They may save your life. Since you are reading this book, you should have learned how dangerous earthquakes can be and that your region suffered one of the strongest earthquakes ever felt in the United States (see Chapter 2). You should participate in the drills and even do better than that: You should become a leader in earthquake prevention for your school and your family. If you do, you have nothing to lose and a lot to gain.

3. I live in California and hear that a strong earthquake is due here sometime. I believe they call it "the Big One." When is the Big One supposed to get here?

At this time (1997), seismologists predict that an earthquake of Richter magnitude 8 or above has a 90 percent chance of occurring within thirty years, most probably along the southern San Andreas Fault, that is, in the area of Los Angeles. Nobody knows exactly when it will hit, but everybody should get ready for its arrival right now (see Chapter 8 for some suggestions).

4. I don't understand how you can "read" when an earthquake occurred in the past by looking at the side of a crack. Can you explain it ?

Soils have been deposited in layers on the surface of the earth over millions of years, either through flows of lava or decomposition of earlier rocks. These layers would look perfectly uniform like those of a many-layered

FIGURE **6.17**

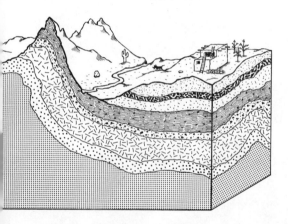

FIGURE **6.18**

FIGURE **6.19**

cake (Fig. 6.17) except that they are distorted by natural disturbances such as floods, erosion, or the mountain building caused by the pushing together of tectonic plates or by earthquakes (Fig. 6.18). That explains why a cut through the earth looks so jumbled. But to date when the events happened, you have to develop a time scale—by knowing, for instance, when a particular earthquake occurred or when a tree was buried (you may have learned that the age of trees can be determined by counting their rings. See Fig. 6.19).

7

CAN ANIMALS PREDICT EARTHQUAKES?

On the night of February 4, 1983, Awilda Salas of Long Beach, California, was sleeping deeply. She was suddenly awakened by the loud chirping of birds in her garden. She could not go back to sleep because the birds kept chirping wildly, but when she eventually did, it was only to be awakened an hour later by an earthquake described in the morning paper the next day as having a Richter magnitude of 5.7 with its *epicenter* in San Diego. (The epicenter is a point on the surface of the earth directly above the focus where the earthquake originates.)

Awilda had never before been awakened in the middle of the night by birds or earthquakes. She firmly believes that on that troubled night the birds had somehow sensed the oncoming earthquake at least one hour before it arrived.

Since time immemorial, people all over the world have believed that animals are sensitive to precursor signals so faint that they cannot be detected even by our best instruments. Two thousand years ago Chinese historians reported strange animal behavior prior to earthquakes, and the Greeks mentioned similar occurrences in 373 B.C.

 ## THE ANIMAL OBSERVATION EXPERIMENT

If you happen to live in an earthquake zone, observe the behavior of your pets or any other animals. Are they behaving unusually? Perhaps they seem agitated, moan or make pained sounds, scratch, and try to run outdoors. These may be advance signals of a coming earthquake, and you should report them to your parents or teachers.

◄◄◄

Not all seismologists believe in the predictive capacity of animals, since no scientific explanations of these uncanny capacities have been given. Yet a German scientist, Dr. Helmut Tribush, intrigued by the stories he heard from the peasants of the Italian region of Friuli after a devastating earthquake damaged or destroyed a hundred thousand houses (including his family home), has dedicated years of research to the question of animal sensitivity to earthquakes. Among the many examples he mentions in his book *When the Snakes Awake* (MIT Press, 1982), the following are typical:

1. A number of witnesses assert that cattle, some of the most placid animals in the world, sense the arrival of

FIGURE **7.2**

FIGURE **7.1**

earthquakes, and have been known to break out of their corrals and stampede (Fig. 7.1).

2. Flocks of birds have been reported flying in circles for hours and then suddenly flying away just before the arrival of an earthquake (Fig. 7.2).

3. Mosquitoes and flies have suddenly disappeared from a neighborhood just before an earthquake.

4. According to reliable witnesses, a few hours before an earthquake devastated an Asian village, cats ran out of every house (Fig. 7.3).

5. Along the southern coast of Hokkaido (one of the main islands of Japan), before the arrival of an earth-

FIGURE 7.3

FIGURE 7.4

quake, thousands of fish jumped into the air, many landing on beaches and dying (Fig. 7.4).

Unlike the myths described in Chapter 6 which blamed animals for causing earthquakes, these reports attribute to animals a higher sensitivity to precursors, those small vibrations unnoticed by humans, allowing animals to predict earthquakes. At present, scientific explanations of these reports are not available and a final opinion on animal sensitivity to earthquakes is not in yet.

But if dogs can follow the smell of a human being, if birds and even butterflies can fly thousands of miles every year from their winter quarters to the same summer quarters (and have made San Juan Capistrano famous because of their return to that California town in the same spring week every year), and if salmon can swim the oceans for months and years and return, thanks to their exceptional sense of smell, to die at the source of the river of their birth, isn't it possible for animals to be particularly sensitive to faint earthquake phenomena?

Earthquake Questions:

1. Why don't adults believe that animals can predict earthquakes?

There is a story told by a reporter who was walking past a stable a few hours before the devastating 1906 San Francisco earthquake. He observed the horses crashing around in their stalls and banging their hoofs against the doors trying to get out. He thought that the horses were simply agitated—he did not understand that some horrendous event was about to take place. Of course, we now know that this happened just before the earthquake, but we can't blame him for not understanding the horses' agitation because animals can't talk and we usually don't understand what they are trying to communicate to us in their own way.

8

SHOULD WE FIGHT OR FOOL THE QUAKES?

Modern buildings are very much like human bodies. They are kept up by the structure, which acts just as the bones of our skeletons do. They are enclosed by their facades, which are like our skin. Their windows are like our eyes, and they breathe through their air-conditioning systems, which act like our lungs. They have an electronic computer system monitoring and controlling their mechanical and electrical operations just as we have a brain in our head controlling our functions (Fig. 8.1). They are built, live a useful life, and eventually die, just as we are born, live, and die.

And just like some of us are hurt in an accident, our buildings are sometimes damaged or destroyed by an earthquake. Finally, just as doctors take care of our health and try to make sure we live longer and better lives, structural engineers design the structures of our buildings to

FIGURE **8.1**

FIGURE **8.2**

stand up for many, many years, and repair them when they become weak due to age or misuse (Fig. 8.2). Engineers must make sure that the structure of a building will support its own weight, the so-called dead load due to gravity, the pull of the earth. In addition, the weight of people, furniture, and all the other movable elements in the building, the so-called live load, has to be supported (Fig. 8.3). Most importantly, the engineer must make sure that the structure will resist the impact of the wind, which may push and pull the building or even twist it during a storm or hurricane (Fig. 8.4). And in the seismic areas of the world, structural engineers have an additional difficult job: They must fight earthquakes.

FIGURE 8.3

In the past, engineers were unable to prevent earthquakes from damaging or destroying our buildings, but they are now beginning to win "the battle of the earthquakes." In the last few years, they have often saved both buildings and lives. How do they do it?

In the preceding chapters, you have seen how we have slowly learned to measure the strength of earthquakes and

FIGURE 8.4

begun to predict where and perhaps soon when it is going to hit. Here are ways in which we can protect our buildings from most quakes by giving them the needed structural strength and flexibility.

Our buildings come in many shapes—to serve as apartment buildings, office high-rises, schools, theaters, sports arenas, churches, jails—and are built with many different materials—steel, reinforced concrete, wood, stone, bricks, or adobe (straw-reinforced mud). All these materials react to the forces acting on them (weights, wind, and earthquakes) in only two ways: They can either be pulled or be pushed.

 ## THE PUSH–PULL GAME

From a thick foam rubber sponge, cut a strip about 150 mm (6 in.) long and 50 mm (2 in.) wide. Grab the ends of the strip and pull them gently. Notice that as the strip stretches, that is, gets longer, its width decreases as if it had been squeezed (Fig. 8.5).

Now place the strip of sponge on its side on a table and push down on it. Notice that it gets shorter and at the same time its sides bulge out (Fig. 8.6).

You have just discovered the two principal actions that a structure experiences, pulling and pushing, or in engineering lingo,

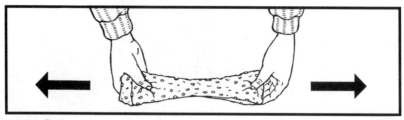

FIGURE 8.5

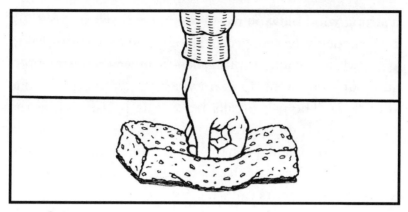

FIGURE 8.6

tension and *compression.* You have also discovered that in the process of being tensed or compressed, the material either squeezes in or bulges out without the volume of the material changing. Of course, a structural material is much stiffer than a sponge so that the lengthening and shortening is very, very small and not visible to the naked eye. For example, the cables holding a suspension bridge are in tension and the columns holding up a building are in compression, but you can't see the stretching or shortening taking place due to the forces acting on them.

◀◀◀

The job of the structural engineer is to make sure that under the forces of the strongest earthquake expected in a seismic area, the materials used for the structure of the buildings in that area will not collapse. To try to achieve this result, all that the engineer must do is satisfy some basic principles.

First, the engineer should avoid making the structure too stiff in the hope of making it strong: a good anti-seismic structure should be flexible. If you have ever seen a strong wind blow on trees, you know that a stiff old oak may suddenly be snapped to the ground by a strong wind gust, while a young sapling bends under the gust's pressure but straightens up again when the wind gust is gone (Fig. 8.7). The oak breaks because it is stiff, while the sapling stands up because it is flexible.

The second and perhaps most important structural principle requires that the material used have a lot of give, a property engineers call *ductility*.

FIGURE 8.7

THE BENDING GAME

Take a piece of chalk and try to bend it: it will snap before you can bend it (Fig. 8.8). Now take a paper clip and bend it back and forth: it will bend a number of times before it breaks (Fig. 8.9).

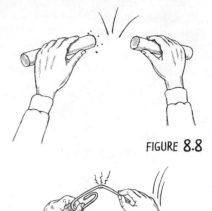

FIGURE **8.8**

We say that the paper clip is *ductile* and the chalk is *brittle* (it behaves like glass that shatters when hit).

You may have noticed that you worked harder to break the paper clip than the chalk, which

FIGURE **8.9**

means you used more energy breaking the paper clip. In the same way, steel absorbs quite a bit of an earthquake's energy before breaking, while concrete breaks without absorbing much earthquake energy.

◄◄

In reinforced concrete, steel reinforcing bars are added to concrete (which is a brittle material) to improve its ductility. If you visit a construction site, this is one reason that you will see many such steel bars set into the columns and beams of a concrete building, especially in a seismic area (Fig. 8.10).

There are, of course, other things that should or should not be done to make our buildings safe from the damaging blows of an earthquake. A building should not be built on weak mushy soil or on soil permeated with water. Such soils

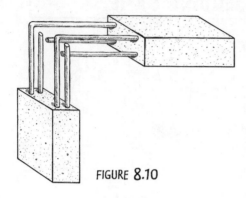

FIGURE **8.10**

develop high friction, slow the speed of the surface waves (see p. 35), and make the buildings bend back and forth much more than when the speedier pressure waves move through rocky soils. The Marina section of San Francisco, that stood on *fill* (soil deposited by humans in shallow water outside the original shoreline) was devastated by liquefaction during the Loma Prieta earthquake of 1992.

Finally, we should not build on the side of a hill unless it has been carefully checked by an engineer to avoid the house being founded on weak soils and possibly tumbling down the hill in an earthquake, as happened in Alaska in 1964 (Fig. 8.11).

FIGURE **8.11**

The importance of these structural principles was shown by the differing behavior of buildings in San Francisco during the Loma Prieta earthquake of 1992. Despite its high 7.1 Richter magnitude, this earthquake did not damage a single skyscraper because they had all been designed in accordance with the most recent requirements of the building codes, the structural laws established by the building authorities that include the principles for safe structures. According to local witnesses, the skyscrapers swayed like trees in a hurricane but were not damaged by the earthquake. Unfortunately, older masonry buildings (bricks joined with cement mortar), which are more rigid, cracked or crumbled from the force of the quake.

In the beginning of the twentieth century, a totally different approach to earthquake resistance was suggested by people who had an understanding of how the property of inertia of a mass could help generate earthquake resistance in a building. They suggested that rather than fighting the earthquakes, it might be easier to fool them! "What about cutting away, or *isolating,* the building from the earth and letting it float while the earth moves *under* it?" they said. "Inertia will prevent the building from moving and the building will not 'feel' the earthquake." (Sounds great but a bit crazy, doesn't it?)

 ## THE ISOLATION GAME

In 1909 a British medical doctor made an ingenious suggestion. "Why not put a layer of lubricating talcum powder between a building and its foundation so that the earth may freely slide *under* the building when an earthquake hits while the building stays put due to its inertia?"

For this game, sprinkle a layer of talcum powder on a sheet of cardboard and place on it a cereal box filled with sand or pebbles to make it heavy and, hence, give it inertia. If you shake the cardboard right and left, the cereal box will slide on it and almost stay put. If the cereal box represents your building and the cardboard the earth's crust, notice that your "building" will move much less than the "earth" and therefore "feel" the earthquake much less. Yet . . . it does not return exactly to its original place, something a real building should always do.

▶▶▶

A more ingenious idea was recently proposed. Why not put the building on springs or on rubber pads?

 ## THE BUILDING ON PADS GAME

To build a model of a building isolated by pads, cut two pads the width of a cereal box from a 50 mm (2 in.) thick soft foam sponge and glue them under the two ends of the bottom of a cereal box (Fig. 8.12a). Glue the bottom of the pads to a sheet of cardboard and fill the cereal box with sand or stones to give it inertia.

Shake the cardboard slightly but quickly and notice that the cereal box will remain practically unmoved due to its inertia; it is partially isolated from the cardboard "earth" and returns *exactly* to its original position (Fig. 8.12b). Note that the sponge seen from the side deforms from a rectangle to a parallelogram (a shape with the top and bottom edges horizontal and the formerly vertical edges slanted).

▶▶▶

A real building is so heavy that it would completely squash a soft "sponge" isolator. Pads used in real buildings are therefore much stiffer and use a sandwich technique with many alternating layers of hard rubber sheets and steel plates (Fig. 8.13). Many buildings in California and Japan are now protected from earthquake damage by sitting on such pads.

Sometimes, when the whole building cannot be isolated (due, for example, to the high expense of isolating a building), parts of the building or its contents can be isolated by suspending them from the frame of the building. The next game will demonstrate this.

FIGURE **8.12a**

FIGURE **8.12b**

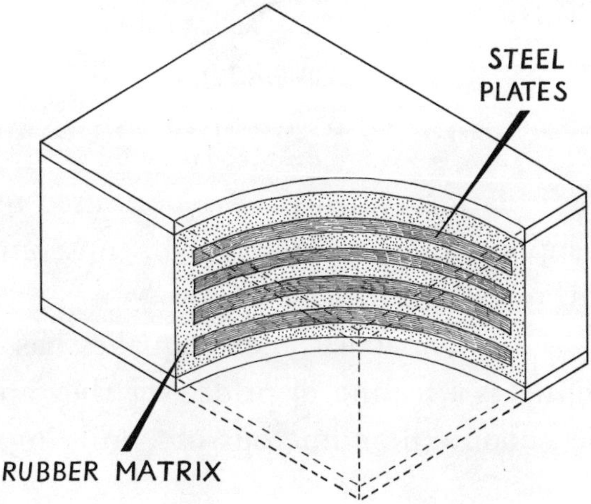

STEEL PLATES

FIGURE **8.13**

RUBBER MATRIX

THE PENDULUM ISOLATOR GAME

Build a "building structure frame" out of cardboard by first taking an empty cereal box and cutting a window on each of its two long sides. Then glue the bottom of the box to a piece of cardboard representing the earth (Fig. 8.14a). Using heavy thread (called button and carpet thread), hang a paper cup (representing, for instance, a computer that you want to isolate) from the top of your building frame and fill the cup with sand or pebbles to give it mass (Fig. 8.14b). If you shake the cardboard, the frame will move but the hanging cup will remain practically unmoved like a pendulum because if its inertia.

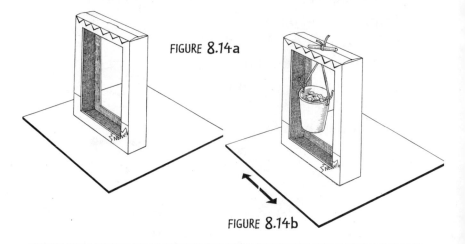

FIGURE **8.14**a

FIGURE **8.14**b

Such "hanging isolating systems" have been used in seismic areas to support fragile sculptures in museums and heavy boilers (Fig. 8.15).

Beginning to tame or fool the earthquakes has given structural engineers a feeling of pride, yet they are still deeply worried about the numerous old buildings that

FIGURE 8.15

were not designed to resist high seismic forces or by now are so run-down they would not survive a strong earthquake. Although *retrofitting* (reinforcing of old buildings) is taking place, mostly in hospitals and other socially important structures, this is a complicated process.

Earthquake Questions:

1. Should I run out of my apartment as soon as I feel an earthquake?

Never—because unless your building were to collapse, you run a much greater risk of getting hurt by some-

FIGURE 8.16

thing falling from the building facade (like a parapet or an ornament), as well as by the street traffic, than you would if you crouched under a strong wooden or metal table and held on to its legs (Fig. 8.16).

> 2. I live in the Los Angeles area. Should I ask my family
> to take precautions against a strong earthquake?

You live in the most severe earthquake zone (zone 4), where the following precautions are recommended to be taken *immediately:*

a) Latch wall and cabinet doors.

b) Store emergency supplies of food and other essentials.

c) Rehearse with your family the emergency plan you chose to enact in the event of an earthquake.

d) Check with the school authorities that similar measures have been taken by them.

You might also suggest to your parents that they take the following additional measures, getting detailed instructions from the local earthquake authorities:

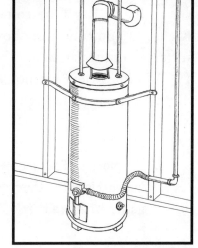

a) Anchor any heavy furniture or piece of equipment (like a chest of drawers, gas water heater, computer, etc.) to the floor or to the studs in the walls, not to the partitions (Fig. 8.17).

FIGURE **8.17**

b) Securely fasten pictures and other heavy objects hanging on the walls or those resting on the floor (Fig. 8.18).

c) Fasten valuable equipment on secure shelves or to anchored tables (Fig. 8.19).

FIGURE **8.18**

d) Have your home or building checked by an engineer to make sure it conforms with the most recent antiseismic code requirements.

FIGURE **8.19**

3. My dad has an office near the top of a tall skyscraper in San Francisco. Is he safe?

If the Big One comes to San Francisco and is of Richter magnitude 8 or above, your father's high-rise may suffer structural damage but should not collapse. The 1992 Loma Prieta earthquake of Richter magnitude 7.1 did not damage any high-rises.

4. My mother told me that Japanese hotels have instructions for their guests in case of an earthquake. What are they?

The instructions—which, incidentally, are valid anywhere in the world—are:

1. Turn off electric appliances (TV, radio, stove, etc.).

2. Stay away from windows.

3. Crouch under a desk or table to protect your head against falling objects.

4. Unlock doors (in case you have to leave in a hurry).

These suggestions are given in case of a serious earthquake. The Japanese take everyday mild earthquakes in their stride.

9

THE SMOKING MOUNTAINS

You learned in the Preface how earthquakes and volcanoes are closely related; you might say that they are cousins, each with its own individuality. The earthquake is secretive and impetuous, acting suddenly without warning; the volcano has a more deliberate and show-off nature, winding up for an eruption and then spitting up *lava* (red-hot melted rock) out in the open for all of us to hear, see, and smell. Yes, there is often the smell of rotten eggs at the time of an eruption (from a chemical called *sulfur dioxide*). And just as there are people with different personalities, not all volcanoes behave the same way. Some may be gentle like Mauna Loa on Hawaii or Mount Etna on Sicily, slowly pouring hot lava out of their *craters* (the hole at the top of the volcanic mountain) so slowly that people can watch and walk away. Others may be violent like Vesuvius near Naples, Italy, or Mount St. Helens in the western United States, suddenly exploding and hurling *bombs* (big boulders), *lapilli* (small stones), and lava dust high into the air and rapidly down the face of the conical mountain—so fast that people don't have time to get out of the way. But, unlike earthquakes, all volcanoes give warning of an impending eruption by rumbling and blowing off steam.

Volcanoes got their name from Vulcan, the Roman god of fire, forge, and hearth, whose "hot" festival was held on one of the hottest days of the year, August 23 (in the Northern Hemisphere). They are born wherever the tremendous pressure of the earth's crust pushes the thick soupy magma of the mantle through cracks in the crust up to the earth's surface as flowing, flaming, slow-moving rivers of lava, or violent eruptions spewing rocks and lava dust into the air. Since this happens mostly along the boundaries of the slow-moving tectonic plates (see p. 2), there is an obvious relationship between the earth-shaking quakes and the lava-spewing volcanoes (Fig. 9.1). In the

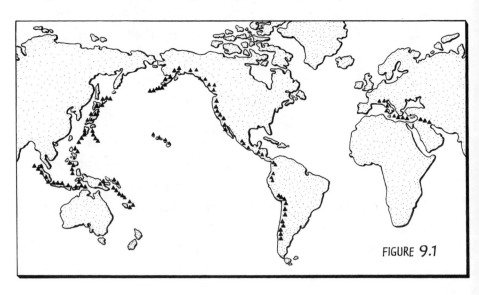

FIGURE 9.1

United States, for example, most volcanoes are found along the area of the West Coast, along which our strongest earthquakes also occur. They are found as well all around the Pacific Ocean, called the *ring of fire,* and along the same strip from Portugal to Australia where earthquakes occur. Look at the maps in Fig. 1.12 and Fig. 9.1 to prove this to yourself.

 ## THE SPEWING VOLCANO GAME

The ideal location to build your own volcano and excite a volcanic eruption—a lava-spewing or a smoking mountain—is either the sandlot of a playground or, even better, a sandy beach along the shore of the sea near a lake or river, where you can build a more substantial volcano with wet sand. If you can't get outside, you can also build a cardboard volcano at home or in school as described on p. 93.

First build a conic mountain of sand (Fig. 9.2) and then get an empty round plastic pill container at least 50 mm (2 in.) tall—the taller, the better (Fig. 9.3a). (Ask your teacher or a parent to get one from a pharmacist.) Make sure the cover of the container is *not* the kind of safety cover that makes it hard for a child to open it, but

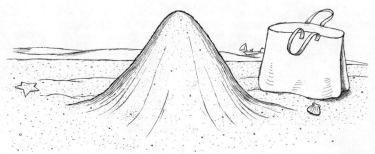

FIGURE **9.2**

the kind that fits tightly on the container without having to be screwed in place. Push the pill container into the top of the volcano so that it's flush with the top, thus opening a *crater* in it (Fig. 9.3b). If you are building a volcano at home, you must first build the cone of the volcano with cardboard instead of sand (Fig. 9.6) and cut a hole at the top to fit in the pill container.

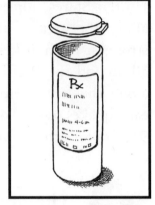

FIGURE 9.3a

Ask a parent or teacher to give you some baking soda, a white powder chemically called *sodium carbonate,* consisting of sodium, hydrogen, carbon, and oxygen. (We are trying to learn a bit of chemistry while having fun.) Ask as well for a bottle of red wine vinegar (a sour liquid consisting of carbon, hydrogen, and oxygen) and a bottle of liquid soap or detergent. Take these to the beach.

First pour a heaping half-teaspoon of baking soda into the pill container and then a few drops of liquid soap or detergent on top of it. Now fill the container with red wine vinegar. A foamy "lava" will spew from the crater and flow down the side of the volcano for a

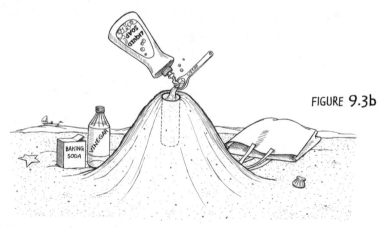

FIGURE 9.3b

while, longer with a larger pill container (Fig. 9.4). (The "lava" erupts because the vinegar is an *acid* and when chemically combined with the baking soda, which is a *base*, it makes *carbon dioxide*, a colorless gas that fills the soap with bubbles and pushes out the "lava.")

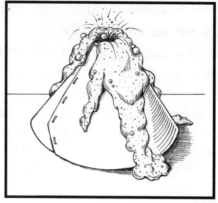

FIGURE 9.4

◀◀◀

There are many volcanoes on the surface of the earth. At present about five hundred are *active,* or alive, and many more are *extinct,* or dead. The *dormant,* or sleeping, volcanoes are by far the most dangerous, because they may sleep for centuries and wake up unexpectedly at any time. Mount Pinatubo in the Philippines had been dormant for six hundred years when it began alerting the local seismologists in 1991 that it was becoming active again by blowing its top and shaking its cone. It erupted violently two weeks later, devastating a wide area not far from the Philippine capital of Manila and killing nine hundred people.

 THE VOLCANIC ERUPTION EXPERIMENT

Build a volcano as described in the spewing volcano game. To excite a volcanic eruption, tightly close the pill container with its cover right after you pour the vinegar in it. The expansion of the gaseous carbon dioxide creates such a pressure in the container that it shoots the cover high into the air, together with drops of the brownish mixture of red wine vinegar and baking soda. It is a dramatic show that, besides shooting up the container cover and the spray mixture, makes a hard popping sound (Fig. 9.5).

Warning: Stand away from the eruption so that the top of the pill container doesn't hit you. Also, if the vinegar–baking soda mixture falls on your clothes or your swimsuit, it will soil them and they will have to be washed.

FIGURE **9.5**

▶▶▶

Since the earth's crust is thinnest under the oceans (see p. 2), you should not be surprised to learn that 90 percent of the earth's volcanic eruptions occur at the bottom of the sea, creating ocean ridges (see p. 9) and, at times, generating horrendous tsunamis (see p. 25). A thousand volcanoes, large and small, have been recently discovered in a relatively small area of the South Pacific.

 ## BUILDING A CARDBOARD VOLCANO

Find a sheet of cardboard, such as a shirt insert, that is about 200 by 350 mm (8 x 14 in.). Take a large compass with an opening of at least 200 mm (8 in.) and with the point of the compass in one corner, draw an arc from the short to the long side: its length is 200 mm (8 in.) (fig. 9.6a). From the point where the arc intersects the long side, draw an arc that intersects the other short side (Fig. 9.6b). From that point to the center of the arc, draw a straight line (Fig. 9.6b).

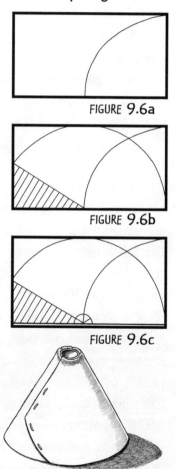

FIGURE 9.6a

FIGURE 9.6b

FIGURE 9.6c

If you do not have a compass large enough to draw the circle, make a compass by tying a pencil to one end of a piece of string that is tied on the other end to a pin at the corner of the cardboard. Adjust the distance between the pin and the pencil so that it is 200 mm (8 in.) long by moving the knot tied around the pencil.

FIGURE 9.6d

Cut the cardboard sheet around the perimeter of the partial circle (Fig. 9.6c).

Draw a circle at the center of the partial circle, about the size of the diameter of the pill container, and cut radial lines from the center to the perimeter of this small circle. Slightly bend down the radial segments.

Bend the cardboard into a cone overlapping the shaded triangle (shown on Fig. 9.6c) and staple it together (Fig. 9.6d). Push down the pill container to fit tightly into the center hole, flush with the cardboard "crater." You have built your cardboard volcano, and you may want to decorate it by painting on its surface light green fields of grass, dark green trees, flows of gray lava, and black rocks. Make the volcano erupt or explode as you would have done with the sand volcano, but do it in a kitchen or bathroom, where you can easily clean up the mess caused by the eruption.

▶▶▶

So far you have only heard of volcanoes' destructive powers, but it would be unfair not to stress the essential role volcanoes have played and still play in the life of Mother Earth. When the earth was born about five billion years ago, volcanoes were everywhere, and by pouring their lava over the earth's surface, they helped to generate the crust on which we live. They then helped to generate the *atmosphere* of carbon dioxide, steam, and other vapors that made possible the life of plants and animals on earth, the only planet of our solar system that deserves to be called "the life planet."

Once volcanoes become inactive and the lava they have spilled on the earth's surface breaks up and decomposes, the result is one of the most fertile soils on earth. Despite our fear of the "smoking mountains," we should be grateful for the bounty they allow us to grow once they have stopped threatening us.

THE SMOKING VOLCANO GAME

After you have built a large outdoor sand mountain (your volcano), using a shovel or your hands, open a horizontal tunnel at its base all the way to its center under the crater, and enlarge it into a cave (Fig. 9.7). Pierce a vertical hole from the top of the cone down to the cave with a stick. Push some moist paper through the tunnel into the cave and put some kindling on top of it. Set the kindling on fire using a lit rolled-up newspaper or a long match. The volcano will blow white-gray smoke out of the crater (Fig. 9.8).

Warning: Do not light the fire without a parent or other adult being present.

FIGURE 9.7

You can also create a smoking mountain at home. Cut a hole in the side of your cardboard cone and set it on a kitchen counter. Remove the pill container and fold back the radial segments slightly to close off the top of the cone.

If you can get a piece of dry ice from a drugstore, push it into the cave of your cardboard volcano and it will blow white smoke for a while. (Dry ice is frozen carbon dioxide, the same colorless gas obtained by mixing vinegar and baking soda, which freezes at a very low temperature and condenses the humidity or vapor in the air into a white cloud that looks like smoke.)

Warning: Don't hold the dry ice with your fingers. Use a towel or prongs.

FIGURE 9.8

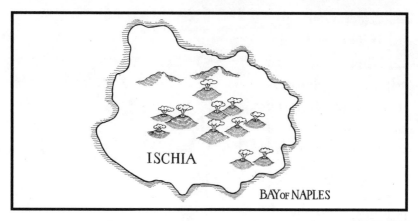

FIGURE 9.9

Volcanoes are also a source of energy that we can use to heat and light up our homes.

The island of Ischia in the gulf of Naples is one of the places on earth dotted with a large number of *fumaroles,* vents in the ground from which steam has been escaping for hundreds of thousands of years (Fig. 9.9). The fumaroles are small cracks in the earth's crust that allow underground water to reach the deep rocks heated by the magma. The heated rocks cause underground water to evaporate into steam, which the Ischian farmers use to warm their tomato plants in winter.

In more recent times the same steam from heated underground water has been exploited for industrial purposes in *geothermal installations.* The first large geothermal energy installation in the world was built in 1904 at Larderello, in Tuscany, Italy, and, recently expanded, is still in use today. It consists of a series of *steam turbines,* engines similar to windmills but turned by hot steam obtained from the upper layer of the earth's crust. The turbines are connected to *electric generators,* the rotating machinery that generates electric power (Fig. 9.10). The Larderello, together with an adjoining geothermal plant, serves the power needs of a large local area and replaces generators run with oil-fed engines, thus saving Italy the need of importing one million tons of costly foreign oil a year.

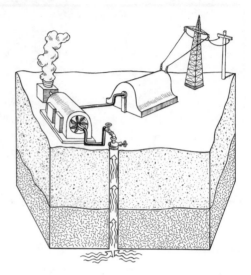

FIGURE **9.10**

In 1995, 1 percent of the electric power in the United States was supplied by geothermal sources (in California and the Midwest). In the near future, 10 percent of the U.S. needs may be met by such sources. Meanwhile, the search for sources of geothermal energy is going on all over the world.

▶ THE GEOTHERMAL ENERGY EXPERIMENT

Note: This experiment should be done with an adult present.

All you need to build a model of a geothermal installation is a tea kettle, a stick or wooden dowel with a 25 mm (1 in.) diameter, aluminum foil, a rubber band, and a small windmill connected to an electric generator that is connected to a small electric bulb. (Tinkertoys® has such a windmill connected with a chain to the shaft of a generator. You can buy it at a toy store.)

Form aluminum foil into a tube about 25 mm (1 in.) in diameter by wrapping it around a stick, folding over the seams and then removing the stick (Fig. 9.11). Attach the tube with a rubber band to the spout of the kettle with the aluminum tube pointing out horizontally. Fill the kettle with water and bring the water to a high boil so that the steam will blow from the kettle spout at high speed. Set the windmill in front of the tube. The blowing steam will make it turn. Switch the generator on and the little bulb will light up.

Warning: To avoid being burned, do not place any part of your body in front of the steam.

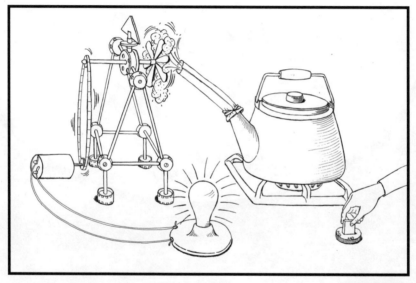

FIGURE 9.11

◄◄◄

Except for the evaporation of the water by the heat of your stove rather than by that of the magma, in physical principles your installation is identical to a geothermal installation.

FIGURE 9.12

Volcano Questions:

1. We live in central Arkansas near Hot Springs. Does the presence of hot springs mean that there is a danger of volcanoes?

Hot springs and geysers are not indications of volcanoes and are actually safety valves that release pressure created when rainwater turns to steam as it seeps down to the hot rocks below the earth's surface. Many hot springs merely flow, while some become geysers, erupting periodically like Old Faithful in Yellowstone National Park (Fig. 9.12).

2. Mount Fuji (Fujiyama) near our home in Japan looks so serene with its snowcapped cone (Fig. 9.13). Is there a danger that it will erupt?

Mount Fuji is a dormant volcano that last erupted in 1707. It could erupt at anytime but will provide warnings by starting to fume and blow off steam and possibly causing earthquakes.

FIGURE **9.13**

IMPORTANT EARTHQUAKES AND VOLCANOES

This list is not meant to be complete or definitive. It is simply the authors' choice of those events that had the greatest impact on the people or the history of the time when they occurred. These events are remembered because they forever changed the environment in which we live.

4600 B.C.

In the western United States there is a chain of volcanoes that dots the Cascade Mountains, stretching from northern California to northern Washington. Near the southern end of this chain is a site that is known in Native American lore as Mount Mazama. It was the site of one of the largest volcanic eruptions in historical times. A 589 meter (1,932 foot) deep depression caused by the collapse of the volcano's cone (called a *caldera*) filled with water and is today called Crater Lake.

1623 B.C.

The Greek island of Thera (also known as Santorini) is located in the Aegean Sea and is believed to be where the mythical kingdom of Atlantis was located. It was the site of a catastrophic eruption that blew off the volcano's cone, leaving only a partial bowl that is today the island's harbor. As a result of the explosion, volcanic ash buried the island's city of Akrotiri and was carried by the wind as far away as Egypt's Nile delta and the shore of Turkey. Sailors lost their ships and farmers lost their crops under the same ash fall. So severe were the changes in the environment that the Minoan civilization, an ancient culture that lived on the Aegean island, collapsed and quickly disappeared.

A.D. 79

Mount Vesuvius on the Bay of Naples, Italy, is the only currently active volcano in Europe. It was known at the time of the Roman Empire as the site of eruptions since antiquity. In A.D. 79, the Roman towns of Herculaneum and Pompeii at the base of the mountain were totally unprepared for the catastrophic eruption that buried them in a shower of deadly cinders. Both towns were forgotten, hidden under a mountain of mud and ash until rediscovered in the eighteenth century by workmen digging a new canal.

1755

On November 1, 1755, Lisbon, the capital of Portugal, was struck by a disastrous earthquake with an estimated Richter magnitude of 8.7 that caused almost all of the city's buildings to topple and a tsunami to roll into the harbor from the ocean, throwing boats onto the land and drowning thousands of the city's inhabitants. After the earth had stopped shaking and the waters from the ocean wave had receded, fires broke out all over the city, totally destroying it. Within a few years the city was rebuilt around a new central square, the Terreiro do Paço.

1815

On the Indonesian island of Sumbawa, there occurred one of the largest eruptions in recent historical times. A huge quantity of ash was thrown into the atmosphere. This ash then circled the earth for the next few years, causing major changes in the weather. In Europe, crops failed because summer never arrived, and in the northeastern United States, it snowed in June, and in the South, there was frost on the Fourth of July. There are eighty active volcanoes on the Indonesian islands. It is not surprising that in 1883 another great eruption caused the island volcano called Krakatau to blow up and disappear under the ocean and a tsunami to move across the Pacific Ocean, killing thousands of people on adjacent islands.

1906

The city of San Francisco lies on one of the longest cracks in the earth, known as the San Andreas Fault. This fault extends virtually the whole length of the state of California. Early in the morning of April 18, part of the crack around San Francisco ripped open, violently shaking the earth with a Richter magnitude of 8.3, knocking down chimneys and brick walls, bursting underground water and gas pipes, and twisting the city's streetcar tracks like pretzels. A series of fires that started after the earthquake caused even greater damage and burned one-third of the city.

1908

The island of Sicily at the foot of Italy is dominated by Mount Etna. Like most of Italy, the island lies in the Alpide belt, a region of heavy seismic activity. The town of Messina, on the tip of the island facing the Italian mainland, was struck in 1908 by the worst quake ever recorded in Italy. The quake, of Richter magnitude 7.5, killed over 120,000 people, most of whom were trapped in the rubble of their masonry houses. Mount Etna is an active volcano that constantly threatens the heavily populated, fertile lands at its base. It last erupted in 1981.

1923

The Japanese are used to feeling the earth shake beneath them, since their homeland is constantly being struck by moderate earthquakes and some strong ones. Just before lunchtime on September 1, 1923, Tokyo, the capital of Japan, was hit by a powerful earthquake of Richter magnitude 8.3 that toppled thousands of lightly built houses, threw down brick walls, caused some buildings to sink in liquefied soil, and gave rise to a tsunami that roared in from Tokyo Bay, washing out bridges and riverside houses. Over one hundred thousand people died because of the quake and from the fires that sprang up immediately thereafter and burned down most of the city.

1964

The strongest earthquake ever to strike the North American continent occurred in the sparsely populated region around Anchorage, Alaska, on Good Friday. Compared to most quakes, which last less than a minute, it was one of the longest-lasting ones, with a duration of almost three minutes. The 8.4 Richter magnitude quake flattened buildings and, because of soil liquefaction, caused houses to topple down hills. It opened cracks in the ground, caused rock slides and mud spouts (where mud shoots up out of the ground like a geyser), and also spawned a tsunami off the Pacific Ocean that was responsible for most of the few casualties.

1976

In the last three thousand years, it is estimated that China has suffered the loss of over thirteen million inhabitants to earthquakes. For this reason, the Chinese have pioneered methods of predicting earthquakes and have achieved some success. For instance, in the province of Liaoning in 1975, people were given warning of an impending quake in time to allow them to leave their homes. But one year later, in the middle of the night, a huge quake of Richter magnitude 7.9 hit the town of Tangshan without warning, trapping thousands of people in collapsing houses and killing an estimated quarter of a million people.

1995

The most recent deadly earthquake occurred quite unexpectedly on a January morning in Kobe, Japan. For years Japanese scientists had predicted that a quake would strike the region southwest of Tokyo. They were taken completely by surprise when a 7.2 Richter magnitude quake hit Kobe, a city southwest of Osaka, almost 420 kilometers (260 miles) away from Tokyo. The Kobe quake caused great damage and loss of life. An elevated roadway in the center of the city fell over on its side as if pushed by a giant hand. Some buildings were squashed, and the port area was a shambles, with huge cracks in piers and fallen structures everywhere. As with most quakes in modern cities, fires erupted as a result of gas leaking from broken pipes. The overall damage proved to be the most costly natural disaster ever.

Earthquakes and volcanoes are becoming increasingly deadly and costly as they hit more densely populated parts of the world. Since some of us live in regions in which there are active volcanoes or where there is a chance of seismic activity, knowing what to expect and how to guard yourself from harm are two lessons we hope you will take away with you after having read this book.

INDEX